NEONS

NEONS

A NOVEL BY

DENIS BELLOC

TRANSLATED BY

WILLIAM RODARMOR

DAVID R. GODINE • PUBLISHER

BOSTON

First U.S. edition published in 1991 by
David R. Godine, Publisher, Inc.
Horticultural Hall
300 Massachusetts Avenue
Boston, Massachusetts 02115

Originally published in France in 1987 by Lieu Commun

Library of Congress Cataloging-in-Publication Data
Belloc, Denis.
[Néons. English]
Neons / by Denis Belloc ; translated by William Rodarmor.—1st U.S. ed.
p. cm.
Translation of: Néons.
ISBN 0-87923-858-5 (alk. paper)
I. Title.
PQ2662.E45466N4613 1990 90–55283
843′.914—dc20 CIP

FIRST EDITION
Manufactured in the United States of America

To Yves Lemoine,
Jacques Blanchier,
Jeannine Estero.
For offered lives.

I ▪

THE SPANIARD

I DON'T REMEMBER anything; she was the one who told me.

"He was big and strong," she said, "with very curly black hair, really good-looking. His name was Joseph, but we called him Jojo.

"I was fifteen when we met, he was nineteen. He worked as a baker but he was crazy about boxing; he boxed as an amateur, he'd even been champion of Poitou when he was eighteen. But he drank a lot, even back then. When he was a baby, they used to mix red wine with the milk in his bottles. His parents used to drink too, and his grandparents, same thing. Whenever he got loaded, he'd yell, 'I'm nothing but a bastard!' and go off to his mother's to sing her a Breton song, always the same one:

From Morbihan to Finistère
You'll find more whores than potatoes there.

"He wasn't too sure who his father was.

"Then I had your brother Alain, and then you two years later. Jojo never worked, just spent his nights in the bars in La Rochelle, and when he came home at night it was a chore to wrestle him up the stairs and into bed. Next morning, he wouldn't remember a thing.

"One day in the middle of winter, he came home bare chested, he had sold his clothes to get something to drink.

"I don't know if he'd been drinking that July night in 1951 at the carnival," she said. "The air smelled of nougat, and gunpowder from the 'Lover's Barometer' stand, and the stink of the trained seals. They were playing popular songs and you could hear the horns on the rides honking.

"A black guy stepped to the edge of the stage, and said, 'C'mon up, feel my muscles, I ain't afraid of nobody. Who wants to box with me?' And Jojo said, 'Hold my coat, I'm going in.'

"So like everyone else, I followed the crowd into the tent. It was very hot, Jojo was wearing shorts, skipping in place to warm up, just like the old days.

"I remember, some kids were yelling, 'Get him, whitey!' I'm sure he was happy to feel the sawdust of the ring under his feet. He won the first round but at the end of the second, I saw the guy smash him in the back of the head. He fell down, staggered to his feet, his nose was bleeding a lot, then the bell rang and I rushed over to hold him up. Walking home, he leaned on me and said, 'Funny, I can't take another step,' and sat down on a stoop in rue des Ménages. People were passing by so he got up and said, 'Come on, they'll think I'm drunk.' Climbing the three flights to our place on rue de La Rochelle, he had to stop at every step. It was an awful night. At six o'clock, he started moaning, his whole right side was paralyzed.

"He went into a coma and died at the hospital twelve hours later. He was twenty-five."

And I was only one and a half. I haven't forgiven him for what he did to me that July night in '51. You left me nothing but a bunch of faded photos, I thought. You ran out on me, you absent bastard. I hate you.

I'M LEANING AGAINST a well in the courtyard of a farm in Sainte-Soulle, there's a fat woman dressed in black, her hair's black too, pinned up in a bun. Standing next to her is a very tall, skinny man with an army cap: old Michaud, the gamekeeper, the husband of the woman in black. Mother says, "Don't be afraid, you'll be happy here with Nounou, you'll see, and there'll be other kids to play with. I'll come every Thursday."

I'm three years old, I hold Alain's hand very tightly.

Jacky and his sister Danielle were there, they came on a winter evening with their bundles of clothes from the welfare people. Then one summer afternoon, Raoul showed up. He dropped his bundle and ran to hide behind a pile of sand between the vegetable garden and the barnyard. We ran after him, Nounou, Jacky, Danielle, Alain, and me. We stopped in front of the sand pile but not too close. Nounou called to him: "Raoul, Raoul. Come on Raoul, don't be afraid." This went on for a long time. She didn't know what to say, so she called, "Here, chicky-chicky," the way she did when she wanted to catch a chicken to slit its throat. Then she tried whistling. Chouquette, the dog, always came when you whistled, but not Raoul. So we went into the house and sat down at the table, leaving a space on the bench nearest the door. And waited. When night fell, he pushed the door open and sat down without a word.

Alain's playing with Jacky. Raoul spends hours crouching out of sight in a corner of the laundry room. Danielle and I are engaged.

We eat potato soup together, and sometimes we walk along the main village street wearing dunce caps with our notebooks on our chests, open to the page with the ink-smudges. On Sundays, we watch Nounou bleed chickens or kill rabbits. Old man Michaud doesn't speak. Ever.

One Sunday Danielle and I get married in the barn. I put a piece of white cloth on her head, Alain and Jacky each hold a corner of her train, Raoul sits watching us from a corner. We walk around the barn slowly, Danielle's holding her doll Caroline, under her arm. "There, now we're really married," I tell her. "You have to kiss me." So Danielle rubs her lips against mine. I take Caroline in my arms and say, "I'm your father now."

And I wait for Mother on Thursdays.

I'm on the lookout.

She rides over on a bicycle, always wearing the same dress with the big printed flowers. In her basket, she brings fish that she buys on the La Rochelle waterfront, and candy too. She hands it out to everybody, even the three other kids.

In Sainte-Soulle, she hides behind the trees. I can't see her flowered dress, I think she's disappeared, and start screaming. She bursts out laughing and kisses me all over, saying, "Mommy loves you."

I don't like this game, I never want her to leave again.

■ ■ ■

Paris has famous specialists who'll be able to cure the disease that's eating away at the muscles in her left arm, so we take a train for Paris. I like the sound of the train. I put my legs on hers and my head on a soldier's thighs. She says, "You'll bother this gentleman." He answers, "That's all right ma'am. Let him be."

I don't think about Danielle or Caroline anymore, the man has a smell I don't recognize. I feel good.

I think I'm nearly seven.

■ ■ ■

There aren't any trees for her to hide behind now, just a sink in the corner and bunks set into the wall, and when the sofabed's unfolded you can't even walk across the linoleum to go piss in the toilet out on the landing.

I'm watching her as she hems curtains for the one window of our furnished room, four yards square, in this hotel on rue Père-Corentin near the porte d'Orléans. I'm waiting but she doesn't say anything, she's too busy and there's a stranger in the room, a Spaniard, I know him a little, I met him two or three times in La Rochelle, he was a friend of Jojo's and I didn't like Jojo's friend: he wouldn't let me ride the merry-go-round at the fair because I talked back to Mommy. What business is it of his?

He's a mason, a lot older than she is, bald and stocky. He always wears a Basque beret. One Sunday they get married. With plastic flowers stuck in their buttonholes.

I'm seven years old.

The Spaniard doesn't drink, but he farts very loudly in the sofabed sheets and he eats noodle soup with a bouillon cube day in and day out, and so do we, and I hate noodle-soup-with-a-bouillon-cube, and he never speaks. When he comes home from his construction site he just plops his ass on a chair, always in the same place, and reads *l'Humanité.*†

"Don't put your elbows on the table pick up your elbow it's your spoon that goes to your mouth not the other way around don't make noise when you eat don't talk at the table you can't go to bed if you don't finish your plate recite your lesson for me

† French communist newspaper.—*Translator's note.*

if you don't know it by heart you can't go to bed." He slurps his soup with his elbows on the table, and he belches after meals.

I say, "I don't like noodle soup and I don't know my lessons." "Shut your face," he answers, but I won't shut it. "Don't talk back to your father," she says, and I think, Shit, he's not my father he's just some foreigner. Why do you always say, "Your father?" And the Spaniard says, "Puta de la Madre de Dios!" Then I know he's going to hit me. He turns red and starts hitting me with his fists, his feet, his boot, or his belt, it hurts like hell, I'm screaming, I know he doesn't like it when I scream, and I bury myself in the sheets of the bunk bed so they cushion the blows and I think real hard, Go ahead, I don't feel anything, you aren't even hurting me, I hate you, you big shit! Exhausted, he stops. I keep on screaming, I want to have the last scream, he says I won't get anything to eat. I don't give a damn. I don't like sitting next to him, he makes me sick to my stomach.

And I don't like noodle soup.

Sometimes she says, "Stop, that's enough! And you, stop screaming!" but I don't hear anything. She can't yell as loud as I can.

▪ ▪ ▪

The school in rue Prise-d'Avesne is boring. I draw women's faces and bodies in my notebooks and textbooks. The hotel room is dark. On Sundays, it often smells of potatoes and rabbit.

Alain learns his lessons by heart and eats all his soup. He lives the absence by keeping quiet.

▪ ▪ ▪

The Spaniard wants a child of his own, so he messes her. She gets big and tired and one day she hits me. She does it all the time, but today, I hit her back. I try to hit her in the stomach.

It's a girl. He names her Adoraçion after his mother and I say, "Boy, what a weird name. Anyway, she isn't my sister, we don't come from the same prick!"

■ ■ ■

I have a son I talk with. The two of us live in the shitter out on the landing and there are rainbow-colored drawers on the walls. My son's name is Michel, don't ask me why. "Hello Michel," I say, "did you do well in school today? Oh good, you got a hundred in arithmetic, that's good my little Michel, you want a bike? But I gave you one yesterday, shit did you break it already? OK, take a million from the blue drawer and buy a blue bike not a red one, and here's ten million to buy yourself a house with, go ahead, see you tomorrow and watch out for cars." And sometimes I scold him: "You haven't been good today, if this goes on you won't get any more presents, all right, I forgive you." Michel and I spend hours together. At home. On Shitter-on-Landing Street.

■ ■ ■

They're bending over the crib that takes up too much room between the bunk beds and the sofa. I'm wiping the steam off the window with my cheek.

Outside, there's nothing to see.

With a chalk, I write in big letters on the wall with the rainbow-colored drawers:

I'M NINE YEARS OLD DADDY IS A JERK.

I'm not going back to the hotel tonight, I swear it. I'm running away.

It's my first night under the neon lights between the porte d'Orléans and Montparnasse. I don't know where I'm going, I'm just walking to get away, following the lights. My satchel is heavy, it gets in my way, I'm cold and a little hungry, I imagine people behind the lit-up windows of apartment houses that aren't furnished hotels. It's like dreaming when you're awake. I don't think of the Spaniard hitting me. Late at night, I sit down on the stoop in front of a doorway in rue Delambre, my satchel in my lap. I want to sleep for a while. A passerby asks, "Are you lost?" "No," I answer, "I'm running away." "Come on," he says, "your parents must be looking for you." He takes me by the hand and leads me to the police station.

The commissaire slaps me. "You little idiot!" he shouts. I don't cry. I don't want to cry. She's there.

"It serves you right!" she says. "Do you have any idea how worried we were, I went to every police station, whatever got into your skull?"

I don't answer, I don't care, I'm not worried and I don't have anything in my skull. Just a big emptiness.

I wait back at the hotel, but the Spaniard doesn't say anything, doesn't hit me. Just as well, I'd have run away the next day.

"He's turning into a real devil," she tells the Spaniard, "I'm going to take him to a psychiatrist to get him straightened out." So she takes me to see him every Thursday. "Draw something," he says, and I draw women's bodies and faces, he asks questions and I answer, "I don't love my father, anyway he isn't my father he's just a foreigner." He asks, "Would you like to have a gun to play with?" and I say, "Sure, but she wouldn't want to buy me one." And he says, "Madame, you might consider putting him in a foster home, his relationship with your husband . . ."

She says to the Spaniard: "I can't believe it, he tells the psychiatrist whatever comes to his mind." She stops taking me on Thursdays.

▪ ▪ ▪

We go to Sainte-Soulle for the summer vacations ("The change will do you good"). We're back at the farm with the well (I'm afraid of the well), and Jacky and Danielle are there. So is Raoul, he doesn't hide as often, just spends hours staring at the dahlias in the garden.

Danielle will be nine soon. She's teaching me to knit. Jacky says I'm a girl. I don't give a damn. I don't like playing cowboys and Indians. He and Alain always want to be the good-guy sheriffs, and I always have to be a dirty redskin, so I'm knitting a muffler for Danielle, and between stitches we talk about George, her new baby. Does he sleep well? Does he drink his bottle? Does he wet his bed? Is he good? Yes, yes, he's very good. Damn, she's calling me for reading.

The book is open on the table, Danielle doesn't know how to read, Nounou slaps her a couple of times, Danielle puts up her hands, Nounou ties Danielle's hands behind the chair and pulls her hair back to uncover her cheeks. Danielle's screaming, Jacky's playing in the courtyard. Raoul's crouching near the dahlias. Nounou doesn't like Danielle. I don't know why.

Caroline, who's just a rag by now, is lying in the corner of the barn where Raoul was sitting the day we got married.

They don't call her "Nounou" anymore, they call her "Mommy."

For two months, the weather's beautiful. Our cheeks turn pink, we've gained weight, she meets us at Austerlitz station.

The Spaniard's waiting at rue Père-Corentin.

■ ■ ■

He broke his wrist on a job. I'm pleased, he isn't able to hit me for three months. The medicine isn't helping the disease in her left arm, they'll have to cut out some of the muscles. I think she hurts a lot. The Chinese woman on the third floor commits suicide. I used to meet her in the stairway when I went to see Michel, she'd smile and say, "Hello, sweetie." We didn't know anything about her except that she was poor and lived alone. Mohammed has disappeared too. He lived with some other Algerians in a tiny flea-ridden shack, and when my mother made crepes, she said, "Mustache, come eat a crepe."

He never spoke, and when he was finished he would smile, which meant thank you. He was old and handsome and had very blue eyes and a mustache which hung over his chin and silver hair, and then some black letters appeared on the hotel walls:

OAS.†

They came on a night like any other night and took Mustache away. The Spaniard read in the newspaper that he committed suicide by jumping from the Vincennes prison tower.

† OAS stands for the Secret Army Organization, a right-wing military group opposed to Algerian independence. —*Tr.*

▪ ▪ ▪

Christmas, but without any toys, just one Christmas tangerine.

▪ ▪ ▪

I ask her, "What's wrong with my left arm?" "That's a skin graft," she says, "you got scalded when you were a baby, so the doctor took some skin from your thigh and put it on your arm. He put the arm between two boards, a splint, but that idiot took it off too soon, so the scar tissue pulled the arm back, you couldn't unbend it. I went to see the surgeon, the one who did the autopsy on Jojo. ('What's a 'topsy?'—'I'll explain some day.') I told him, 'You have to operate on my son so he can stretch his arm out.' And the surgeon said, 'All right, I'll cut the scar tissue, it's nothing, I can operate without putting him to sleep, kids of that age don't feel any pain.' So I jumped up and smacked him across the face and yelled, 'You damned well better put my son to sleep!' and slammed the door behind me. He operated without putting you to sleep, but when he'd see me in the street he'd cross to the other side. Anyway, now you can stretch your arm out."

It looks a bit like a map. It's a little ticklish. I enjoy stroking my left arm.

I find the map in my geography book: Africa. I take a trip around the graft with my finger. Rabat, Dakar, then it fades away toward the elbow, the Atlantic Ocean, let's say. I move up to Djibouti, Tunis, Algiers. The wrinkles between Algiers and Rabat are the Strait of Gibraltar. Toward Spain.

At Shitter-on-Landing Street, I've rubbed out the rainbow-colored drawers. Michel doesn't exist anymore, I don't remember when he died.

I'm ten already.

■ ■ ■

We've left the furnished hotel for a caretaker's apartment on avenue du Maine. It's a bit bigger, with a separate kitchen and a toilet out in the courtyard. I sort the mail in the afternoons after school and I get up at dawn on Thursday mornings to wipe the floors while she sweeps the stairs and I say, "Good morning, ma'am" and "Good morning, sir" and "Excuse me" when I'm in the way and they're trying to get in or out of their two- or three- or even five-room apartments with toilets that aren't out in the courtyard.

The Spaniard hits me harder now, it's only fair, I'm getting bigger and tougher. At school on rue Asseline I hit the kids too, I grab them by the neck and ask, "What's that you said, you asshole?" They answer, "But I wasn't even talking to you," then I punch them and yell, "Shut your trap, you little shit, I don't like people talking back to me!"

In class, I don't do a damned thing, just draw women's faces and bodies in my books.

At our place on avenue du Maine, guys from Spain sleep over for two or three nights while they look for somewhere to stay. They're running away from Franco.

He's tall and elegant, with a handsome face. "I was a Spanish teacher in Madrid," he says. "I'm leaving for London tomorrow to be with my wife and two daughters."

He's asleep on a makeshift bed. I'm not in the apartment

anymore, he's holding my hand and smiling at me without speaking. He's the absence. My belly's quivering and I feel good. I feel like kissing his cheek, but that would wake him up. Then the dream fades, and I'm left with a big emptiness in the pit of my stomach. I hate his daughters.

■ ■ ■

Every Thursday, in the Luxembourg gardens, I peek at the statue of the naked young man sitting on his left heel. Seeing his penis between his outspread legs bothers me but I don't know why.

One day, in the Luxembourg pissoir, I see the prick of a man pissing and it bothers me the same way, but my heart is beating very fast.

There's a pissoir on the way to school, next to the cemetery wall in rue Froidevaux. It's dark already. I set down my satchel in the pissoir, I just want to see a man's prick to make my heart start beating fast again. The guy's wearing a cap, I can't make out his face too well, he takes my prick in his hand and it swells and stiffens, my chest is pounding, he shakes it in a funny way, I feel like I'm pissing but it's different, it feels good when it comes out, I touch the end and it's sticky.

I pick up my satchel and walk out of the pissoir, with the man with the cap and the sticky end all mixed up in my mind. I run back to our apartment, sweating and shaking a little.

That night, my geography lesson flies to pieces in my head and the Spaniard punches me with all his might. I dive under the sheets and scream like I've never screamed before and I jerk my prick thinking hard of the man in the cap and the cap turns into a Basque beret. I imagine it's the Spaniard's hand and his hand makes me piss. I soak the sheets, I'm all sticky.

I'm eleven years old, I don't know who I am, and I don't piss the way the others do.

Now I set my satchel down in the pissoir on my way to school and on the way home, I get jerked off and I jerk them off, sometimes they suck my prick but I don't want to suck theirs. I think putting their pricks in my mouth is dirty and I don't want them to kiss me, I don't like their breath. I say, "I live next door, I'll be in front of the building at such-and-such time" (I can always find some errand to run) and we go over to rue Vercingétorix behind a fence in front of a torn-down building, I shake their pricks and I piss with pleasure. The guy often shows up in the pissoir after lunch, he gives me money when I make him come, so I buy Mistral and Malabar candies and give them out to the kids I've chosen.

I learn the looks and the gestures that attract the men who wait near the pissoir when the Cinéac at Montparnasse station lets out, and I go to the Texas movie house on rue de la Gâité with her, I jerk off a man sitting next to me and she doesn't notice a thing.

I flunk the exam to pass into sixth grade. No big deal for a kid from a poor family. In any case, I can't remember anything anymore.

It's Thursday evening, I'm doing the shopping in rue de l'Ouest with my string bag in my hand and a list in the pocket of my shorts. 1 kilo of potatoes, 1 head of lettuce, 1 kilo of bananas ("Not too ripe, the cheapest ones they have"). A big guy with a very black mustache is standing at the other end of the pissoir. I look at my neighbor's prick but it doesn't turn me on, I like the man with the mustache better, so I leave the pissoir and go to rue de l'Ouest, where the greengrocers are. It starts raining hard, I take cover in the entrance to a building, he catches up with me and says, "You're a good-looking kid, maybe we can get together sometime. Let me look at my datebook." But it isn't a datebook, it's a wallet. He opens it and shows me a card with two red and blue lines, and says, "Police. You're coming with me," and I start to shake and sweat, I want to run away but my legs are all numb, he asks:

"Have you been doing this for long? How old are you?"

"I'm twelve and a half."

"Got any I.D. on you?"

I pull out my family discount card.†

"Your parents know what you're up to?"

"Oh, no, sir!"

"All right, listen: I want you to scram, and if I ever catch you in there again, I'm taking you in."

He leaves, and I stand there panting.

Back at the apartment, she says, "Shit, you forgot the bananas." That night, I learn my lesson by heart and I don't go near the pissoir for two whole months.

I don't want to wear shorts anymore, I want long pants.

▪ ▪ ▪

The Spaniard rips the sheets off the bunk bed and catches me thumbing my nose at him, he goes berserk, he's punching

† A card issued to the members of families with three or more children—*Tr.*

me like a boxer, I don't cry, it hurts too much, he grabs me by the neck and boots me out into the courtyard.

I don't know if he'll ever stop hitting me and I don't care.

I'm thirteen. I live an enormous loneliness.

▪ ▪ ▪

For Mother's Day, I give her a wooden picture with the heads of a doe and a horse burned in, I made it at school for her.

"That's very pretty, you've got talent," she says. "Let me show you something." Rummaging under a pile of laundry in the closet, she pulls out some notebooks. They're full of drawings of women's faces and bodies, some of them in color, there are even queens of France wearing pearl necklaces. "When I was young, I used to draw, too," she says, "but since Jojo died I haven't had the heart."

One day, she buys a box of oil colors and paints a picture of the La Rochelle harbor. The sea in the painting is very rough, but the sky is pure blue. There aren't any clouds.

I go upstairs to the sixth-floor tenant's place with her, she cleans for him once a week. I like going with her. It's a big apartment, three rooms with books and knick-knacks everywhere, not just seashells like in our place. But mainly, it has a bathroom, all white. It's the first time I've been in one. I sit on the edge of the tub and wait until I feel like pissing. Then I drop my shorts and sit on the toilet. I sit up very straight, hands on my knees, pretending it's a throne. I point my prick toward the center, so I can hear my pee hit the water. I stand up slowly, taking care not to leave a single drop on the edge of the black bowl, and pull the chain.

I wouldn't mind hanging the painting of the La Rochelle harbor on the bathroom's white wall.

▪ ▪ ▪

I'm sick and tired of grade school, I better not screw up on the certificate test, and I pass the bastard. I want to be a sailor and go to sea, but she says: "No way you're going to run off to Saint-Mandrier (the training school for cabin boys), you're going to learn a real trade. That way you'll get a good job, and when you get married, you'll be able to raise your kids decently." I can't tell her that I get married and jerk off my kids in rue Froidevaux every day. The Spaniard says, "Work in the building trades is a good job and you make plenty of dough doing contract plastering," so I apprentice myself as a plasterer.

One, two, three . . . fourteen: today's the day I turn fourteen.

By borrowing a lot of money, we trade the caretaker's apartment for a wooden shack with a yard in the suburbs at Fontenay-sous-Bois, it's goodbye to the whirlwind years.

There's a body in the rue Froidevaux pissoir next to the cemetery wall. A wild child's corpse.

His name was Michel.

▪ ▪ ▪

The Spaniard stops hitting me, I'm bigger than he is now. He's fixing up the shack. "Later on, I rebuild it solid." His daughter's dowry.

Alain got thrown out of school, so he's learning food service in a butcher-shop in the 16th arrondissement, and I'm dirtying my hands and my hair with plaster and gravel, warming lunch-buckets, and sweeping up job sites after proles who start their mornings with coffee and brandy.

"Damned if I didn't pork the old lady good last night!"

White wine at the ten o'clock break.

"That bitch forgot the pâté again!"

Red wine at noon.

"Hey, faggot, you forgot to clean my tools!"

More brandy and coffee after lunch.

"Hey, kid, what are you up to? Better stop beating your meat at night, it'll rot your mind."

Afternoons, I catch the bus home to the shack at the Château de Vincennes stop. There are pissoirs in the park. I'm leaning against a tree, the guy wants to kiss me, I struggle a little, he forces my lips apart, I search his mouth with my tongue, kiss him on the cheeks, the neck, the eyes, stroke his hair hard, my eyes are full of tears and I come, trying not to scream. We separate without saying a word and I'm left with that big emptiness in the pit of my stomach.

Back at the shack, they're saying we have to fight for our rights, and struggle against the capitalists who exploit us. They talk about the Popular Front, paid holidays, the war in Spain, the Nazis, and then October 17 and the great Russian people, Lenin, Cuba, the GDR, the *Internationale*, communism, syndicalism. Alain and I join the Young Communists, the Communist Party, the C.G.T., we spend our time informing, organizing, and recruiting. We hawk *Nous les garçons et les filles* and *Huma-Dimanche.*†

It's nighttime, Alain and I are walking back from a cell meet-

† C.G.T. is the *Confédération Générale du Travail*, France's main leftist national trade union. *Nous* and *Huma-Dimanche* are left-wing publications. —*Tr.*

ing. "I'm scared, bro'," I mutter to him. "Don't worry, little guy, they're just rich assholes." He pulls a jimmy from under his jacket and forces the hardware store's door. He's used to this, I tell myself, it can't be his first time. Then I'm not afraid anymore, I get very excited . . . I pull open the cash register, take the change and piss in the drawer, climb onto the counter, drop my pants and take a dump, then smear the shit on the walls.

Back home, we stash the loot under our beds.

I'm fifteen, I don't understand a thing about dialectical materialism, and I don't give a rat's ass for the class struggle. I don't even care for my own class.

We break into a Prisunic supermarket, a penny arcade, a restaurant, I piss and shit and smear shit on the walls, writing:

ASSHOLES SCUMBAGS FUCKHEADS PIGS.

One morning, she finds our stash. She screams questions at me, we confess everything, except the shit. The Spaniard isn't there, he's gone to work, so she picks up a chair and lets me have it three times, I don't fight back, on the fourth time she passes out in a heap, we slap her to wake her up, she looks like death.

"You're coming with me to the police station," she says, "I don't have any choice." So we go with her. She's put on her best Sunday coat, we're walking single file, with her in front.

"These are my sons, they're burglars," she tells the cops. "Do whatever you have to." She walks out without turning around.

Alain whispers a few words to me: "I'll take all the blame, don't worry, little guy."

Second precinct: the cops want to know about everything,

even the shit; I don't tell them anything about the shit. Their fingers pound the typewriters, typing out statements I sign without reading.

Conciergerie prison: I bend over to show my asshole. Nothing up there. Jail cell. Vital statistics.

Examining magistrate: "I think you can be rehabilitated. I'm sending you to a work camp for juvenile delinquents."

▪ ▪ ▪

Each of the dorms is named for a different province: Alsace, Poitou, Lorraine, Bretagne, Provence, as if to make the kids feel they've taken a trip. There's a machine shop, workshops for masonry, painting, gardening, and no walls, just counselors. At Savigny-sur-Orge, I'm a Lorrain in a grey outfit, stacking bricks in the masonry shop.

Robert's thirteen, he's tall and skinny, I don't know what he's in for. He never talks, doesn't smile either, just walks along staring at his shoes. He's a Lorrain, like Henri, who is someone I do know, we were in grade school together, in the certificate class. Henri's in for stealing a car, he's fifteen and big already.

He tells Robert, "Suck me off or I'll beat you up." So Robert sucks Henri off, and Henri says, "He'll suck you all off, but you gotta slip me a pack of smokes."

At night, after the Swiss chard, the guys from Alsace, Poitou, Bretagne, Lorraine, and Provence all line up outside of Robert's room.

I get caught talking during roll-call, and they nail me for it. The cell has very high mud-colored walls, and way at the top, a tiny window that hardly lets in any light. You shit in a hole and sleep on a plank bolted to the wall.

I put on a grey canvas outfit and leave my clothes and boots outside the cell door, which opens three times a day for chow and once in the evening for blankets. I spend five days talking to myself, anything that comes to mind, singing too, but mainly beating off. A couple of times a day. It's more difficult the third time, you have to think harder. And my prick becomes an element apart from my body, an independent life.

■ ■ ■

FRESNES PRISON
Censor No. 16

Little bro':

Thanks for your note. It hurts I feel responsible because I got you into this.

Keep your chin up it'll be over soon. It's up to us to be happy. Everything's cool here.

Don't give up I'm not forgetting you.

Alain

■ ■ ■

She visits the camp twice, brings chocolate and cookies and new underpants. "I can't come more often," she says, "I go see your brother at Fresnes every week, and I'm worn out." I share the chocolate and the cookies with Robert, the underpants are much too big for him.

The counselors ask me if I want to go back to my parents, I

say anything but the shack, the stepfather, and the brandy-coffee-white-wine-red-wine proles, so they suggest a camp out in the provinces where I can learn another trade ("Anything you like, anything at all, and there's no solitary there.") Without hesitating, I say yes, so long as it's far away. Very far.

She won't let me go. ("He'll just get into trouble and besides, he has to finish his apprenticeship.") So I was a Lorrain for four months for nothing. I should have run away, jumped the non-existent walls. My fingers, their nails white with plaster, melt into the shadows of the Vincennes park pissoirs.

▪ ▪ ▪

Adoraçion looks like her mother. At eight, she hates the Spaniard who never kisses her, never talks, who reads *l'Humanité* with his ass on a chair, always in the same spot.

She becomes my sister then.

Alain gets released seven months after she found our stash. "Stop it, let him go!" I scream, "it isn't worth it." And I pry my older brother's hands from around the Spaniard's neck, I was afraid the old guy would croak. I don't know why Alain wanted to kill him, he didn't explain, left without a word, living his absence somewhere else. I run into him at times. He's often drunk, says he's shacked up with a whore and that at night he takes a switchblade and mugs queers in Vincennes park. He tells them, "Hand over the money you dirty faggot, or I'll stick you." One night, he gets nabbed by the cops. I miss him.

My apprenticeship is finished. I've learned a trade, the old shack is "built solid" for an old couple and their daughter "when she gets married and has kids." It all makes me want to puke.

Alain gets out of Centrale prison, starts prowling the streets of Fontenay-sous-Bois. He pulled sixteen months, long enough for his body to get covered with tattoos: a crucifixion, a picture of the open road, two clasped hands, a cobra, an owl, an eagle, a poem to his mother, the name of some whore, and three dots on the back of his hand.

I've been living since I turned seventeen.

■ ■ ■

"You wanted to be on your own," the Spaniard spits at me, "now you got it, get the fuck outta here, this house ain't yours anymore, you're no son of mine, I never want to see you here again!" Laughing, I yell that I don't give a fuck about his shack, he's never been my father, he's just a shit and he'll always be a shit. He comes close, I feel he wants to hit me. He's red in the face, he stinks of hate. I tighten my fists. If he hits me, I'll destroy him. "Watch it," he sputters, "I'm not as young as I used to be, but I can still teach you a lesson."

"Just try, fuckhead, go ahead, you hit me and I'll smash your face into the wall!"

He doesn't say anything, just chickens out, he's a dishrag. I laugh because he's scared, he's always been scared, and because I'm jumping the fence. I'm going to breathe free.

■ ■ ■

For the time being, she finds me a one-room place at the Etournettes hostel run by Father Marouen. It's got counselors, a dining hall, and Roland. We met in the dining hall, over an exchange of looks. "I saw you come in yesterday," he said, "you looked out of it." We went up to his room, he put his hand on my hip. "I'd love to go to bed with you." I laughed. "I never do it with guys my own age," I said, "and I've never gone to bed with anyone, I always do it standing up." He didn't push it, just sat down at his table in front of a mirror and started to rub foundation makeup on his face and brush mascara onto his eyelashes. "I have a lover who supports me," he said, drawing a white line around his lips. "I'll introduce you to him." He looked at himself in the mirror, and let out a few squeals. "Would you like me to make you up?"

I wait for evening to cover my face with makeup and lengthen my lashes. I'm wiggling my ass and squealing with Roland. There are other painted faces between Clichy and Pigalle, the masks of queens, whores, and bums, but in the neon glare of the boulevard and the sharp stink of the pissoirs I'm all alone: the absence wearing makeup.

We drink a few kirs at the bar in a hangout on rue Dancourt; it's Roland's headquarters, where he meets his lover. I have Lucien the bartender in the phone booth, Roland's lover Pierre buys me a drink.

Pierre squeezes some Vaseline onto his fingers and smears it on my ass, rubs it in, and shoves his prick between my cheeks. It's like being burned, I claw at the pillow so as not to cry out, he pumps in and out a long time, and comes inside me, moaning. "Did I hurt you?" he asks. "A little," I answer, "it's my first time." He apologizes, "I'm really sorry, when I saw you, I thought . . ." I tell him it's nothing, that I really liked it, so he says, "Make a wish! When it's the first time, you always have to make a wish." We burst out laughing. My makeup has stained the pillow, and my mascara's running.

It's nighttime, over by boulevard d'Anvers. Something doesn't feel right between my legs, like the opening was enlarged with a scalpel.

The motorcycle's up on its kickstand. It's black and white, and the chrome is farting sparks. I climb aboard. I want to eat miles of neon lights on it. Instead, it leads me straight to the pigs.

I left the Spaniard a month ago.

■ ■ ■

I bend over again, show my asshole again. I'm afraid they'll notice something. I feel as if my hole is invading the Conciergerie basement.

I stretch out on the cell floor. There's just one bench and it's occupied by other delinquents' asses. I try to sleep, try to forget the lights they never turn out.

The door opens and closes, some guy starts pounding me on the back:

"Son of a bitch little bro', what are you in for?"

"I stole a bike. You?"

"Smashed up a hot car, no driver's license, the shits."

I'm not sleepy anymore. Lying close together, we dredge up old times. He's the one who remembers: Sainte-Soulle and my marriage ("We bust a gut laughing, me and Jacky, you two looked so serious."), rue Père-Corentin ("What a shit-hole, it was so depressing, you wanted to puke.") and then avenue du Maine ("With your dustrag in your fist, little bro', you really looked like an asshole.").

In the morning, he brings up Jojo's death. He was there at ringside, it's his only real image, it's glued to his retina. He admits he was a rebel inside long before the furnished hotel, says he wanted to grow up just so he'd look like the image. Then he falls silent, leans his head against the wall and closes his eyes. I doze off.

"Why don't we switch clothes?" he suggests. "I'll make a better impression on the examining magistrate." So I pull on his too-tight black pants, his black leather jacket and his boots, which are black as well and too pointy. He slips into my grey trousers, my pea jacket with anchors on the buttons and my shoes that buckle on the side.

They ship us off to Fresnes in the same prison van.

We get undressed, drop our rags on a counter.

He's standing in front of me, naked. He looks like the faded photos (wearing boxing shorts, leading with his left) the nose, mouth, shoulders, fists. Especially the fists. But not the hair. The hair is hers.

Our assholes to the guards. He's rolling his shoulders, flexing the tattooed eagle's wings.

We put on grey jumpsuits and brown shoes, stick a pair of sheets and a blanket under our arms. He heads for cellblock three, me to number two. He turns around and gives me a wink, trying to look cheerful.

He's only just turned twenty. I wish the walls would blow up.

▪ ▪ ▪

There's a huge guy in cell 391, and he introduces himself. "They call me Big Duduche, I punched out a pig. Whenever I'm loaded I always punch out some pig. What are you in for?" I tell him, but he doesn't think getting busted for stealing a bike is exactly the big time. I don't give a damn, I have to take a shit like crazy and there isn't anything between the cell and the shitter. I'm thinking of the smell.

Didier shows up three days later. He just got out of the hole: eight days for squealing on the former tenants, who tried to bugger him. The would-be buggers got fifteen days. Big Duduche doesn't have much to say except, shit, he could sure use a stiff drink. Didier talks about his father who's in business in Madagascar. They never see each other, it's just as well, they can't stand each other. Didier stole some wheels so he'd get sent up, to piss off his old man, but his father ("that asshole") couldn't care less, and his mother ("that bitch") split long ago. Didier's a pain in the butt.

In the yard, we play blindman's buff with belts. The guards are real motherfuckers, they beat us up if we don't play. At night, we sing songs about the Tataouine stockade. †

Didier's lying on his bed, giving himself a hard-on. "Isn't my prick pretty?" he says. I want to touch it, but he says, "No sirree, I'm going to beat my meat while thinking of some cute girl's ass."

Didier's a fucking asshole. We jerk off in turn, so as not to set the bunks shaking.

We stand in a circle around Didier and Doe-Eyes (he has lines tattooed at the corner of his eyes). He's the former tenant, the bugger. Didier tries to duck, but Doe-Eyes slugs him hard, his fists all over his face, and drops him in a corner of the exercise yard. Didier's nose is pissing blood, nobody wipes it off.

I pass Alain pushing a meal cart, he has more tattoos on his

† A military prison in Morocco.—*Tr.*

hands, he asks how's it hanging, little bro'. Everything's cool, I tell him.

Duduche tattoos the patron saint of thieves on my left arm. I don't think of the absence anymore.

■ ■ ■

FRESNES PRISON
Censor No. 3

Denis:

I got your letter today thank you. Yes, I know you've been arrested. Where will you go when you get out? No way you can come here.

I've given up on you two. You wanted freedom, but it's too noble a word for you.

Don't write me anymore. Wait until you're a man, and don't think about me.

May 1968 be better than 1967.

Mommy.

■ ■ ■

I stick Didier's head down the shitter and flush it, he's screaming that I'm out of my mind but I yell, "I want him to shut his trap." I'm squeezing his throat with my hands, he turns blue, starts to drool and moan. I tighten some more, I want him to die. Big Duduche hits me to make me let go.

Duduche gets out of the slammer, and the municipal court hands Didier six months. I'm paroled one January evening. It's dark and cold, all I've got in my pocket is three francs twenty and Duduche's address in Saint-Maur-des-Fossés. I catch a train for Paris. Alain's probably asleep.

At the hostel, Father Marouen screams, "I don't want any ex-cons around here! Beat it, you creep." My stomach's in knots, I'm so angry. "You know, God the fucking Father, you've got a real prick working for you!" So I set out to walk all the way to Saint-Maur. Hands in my pockets, I don't even see the neon lights, I just walk without stopping. The water in the pissoirs between Clichy and Pigalle must be frozen.

Big Duduche says he can't put me up because of his folks, and sends me over to one of his buddies, Dédé the Outlaw. Outlaw just did two years in the Santé prison for robbery, and he's violating his parole by being in Paris. His place is really gross: a mattress, a sink, and empty beer bottles and cigarette butts everywhere. I collapse onto the butts and fall asleep.

Outlaw says he can't pay the rent anymore, he doesn't want to get sent up again for violating his parole, he's sick to death of this godforsaken place. "Why don't we get the fuck out of here? Maybe go to the seaside, whaddya say, huh?" I think the seaside in winter must be neat, so we steal a 2 CV Citroën and split for Saint-Malo.

Big Duduche, Outlaw, and me.

We run out of gas, so we steal another car. Outlaw opens the doors and hot-wires it with a nail file. We swipe food from fruit stands and pick up butts when they're long enough and not too filthy. We sleep in the car or in barns.

The old walls of Saint-Malo face the sea, it's practically the ocean. The tide is out, so we stumble around in the mud and suck on a couple of limpets. Outlaw suggests we head north. "Let's go all the way to Sweden, and never set foot in France again, this country's fucked. Up there, we'll screw big blondes with asses like this." So we make our way north along the coast, hitchhiking when the car runs out of gas in the middle of nowhere. Le Havre, Dieppe, Calais, Boulogne, Dunkerque. We walk across the border into Belgium without going through customs because Outlaw's lost his ID card. We decide to make for Furnes, swipe some wheels, then head for Ostende. There's nothing but dried fish in the stands along the way to Furnes and we're starved. We haven't had anything to eat besides fruit and raw vegetables since Saint-Maur, and we're sick of it. I took my last shower while I was still in Fresnes, and we wonder if we'll ever be able to peel off our socks and underwear.

There isn't enough gas in the heap we stole in Furnes, so we decide to hit up the nearest burg for a reliable, comfortable set of wheels. We find a nifty white Citroën D.S. on the Bruges market square and roar off to Ostende. That night, we park the D.S. in a dead-end alley near the waterfront and lower the front seats so we can stretch out. We don't notice the cop car with its lights out blocking the alley, just see the guns through the windows of the D.S. Far out; we'll finally get something to eat.

Back to Bruges. This time, it isn't the Conciergerie prison: we don't have to show our assholes, just sign a warrant, pay a lightning visit to the judge, then jail: cell 97. It's rustic and clean. Nine-foot ceilings, an old wood table black with age and a stool to match, a pull-down wooden bunk with a sack of horsehair for a mattress. No running water: just a pitcher, a stone sink, and a bucket to crap in, with a few pages from a magazine to wipe your butt with. The window looks out on a canal with people walking along it. Something's bothering me, and I look around to find out what. It's the crucifix on the wall. I toss it out between the bars.

The scene's cozy and the food's good, French fries with mayonnaise once a week. A fat priest, old and ugly, comes by on Fridays: "Believe in God, my son." "Oh yes, sir, you couldn't get me a pack of smokes, could you?" So he brings a pack from Saint-Michel. I can't bring myself to say, "Father."

I do piecework in my cell, folding handouts advertising a line of lawnmowers. That way, I can hit up the canteen for soap, writing paper, and especially toilet paper. *Point de Vue—Images du monde* is rubbing my ass raw.

The judges sentence us to four months, and the absence comes back. I cut its image out of magazines: handsome men, not too young, wearing suits and ties. I look at them at night in my bunk, beating off with my eyes closed, but not too fast, to give the picture life.

▪ ▪ ▪

Denis:

Don't be surprised I haven't answered your letter. I'm very tired. If you come back around here I have 150 francs for you from the building trades paid holidays fund.

Thanks for the Mother's day card.

Mommy

P.S. The judges sentenced you to eight months in jail for stealing the motorcycle.

▪ ▪ ▪

Outlaw set his cell on fire, he wanted a view of the canal. Now that he's in the hole, he doesn't have any view at all. I practically bust a gut laughing.

▪ ▪ ▪

FRESNES PRISON
Censor No. 13

Little bro':

So you're in jail again. I want you to stop fucking up and get a job when you get out. Don't follow in my footsteps. If you only knew how sick I am of these bars. Promise me you'll try to straighten out. I'll help as much as I can.

Let's write each other more often.

Your brother who loves you,
Alain

▪ ▪ ▪

I say goodbye to the passersby along the canal, and we leave Bruges on a beautiful spring day. A night in the Mons jail, and in the morning, the Flemish badges hand us over to the French ones.

We're taken to the Interpol office in Maubeuge. Fingerprints, rap sheet, I get socked with the whole eight months. It takes hours. A cop says all right, you can go, you've got eight days to get out of the département. We hit the road for Paris, but no stealing cars: this time, we're hitching. I find some wire to wrap around my shoes to keep the soles from flapping; my pea jacket has lost all its buttons with anchors on them.

We pick fruit from trees, razz Outlaw about his Swedish girls with asses like this, Big Duduche dreams of a good stiff drink. We stock up on butts when we cross a big town, and sleep in barns.

A car picks us up outside of Paris and takes us as far as Saint-Maur. Big Duduche wants to go back to his folks, so he says, "So long guys, come see me one of these days." Outlaw and I push on to Fontenay-sous-Bois. I wait a few yards from the shack, now rebuilt in brick. It's market day, and she comes out wheeling a shopping cart. I wave to her, but she doesn't recognize me at first. Then she says, "You're a mess! What are those things on your feet? Hold on." From her purse, she takes out 150 francs and the money order stub. Says she's been carrying it all this time in case I showed up.

I ask her how she's doing. "Not too good," she answers. "Alain's in prison in La Rochelle for armed robbery and assault, I don't know if he'll ever get out. What was he doing in La Rochelle, anyway? And what about you? Where will you go?" I tell her I have no idea, me and my buddy will have to see. She tears a scrap from her shopping list, writes her phone number on it. "Call me if you need help," she says. "Good luck, big boy!" We kiss each other and I watch her as she walks away; her cart's empty, but it seems very heavy.

I buy a pair of marked-down shoes, a Camembert, a liter of red, two baguettes, and we head down to Vincennes. We plop our butts on a bench next to the park and wolf down the bread. The wine makes us dizzy. We buy Gauloises with the rest of the money, and walk back up along Vincennes and the rue Faubourg-Saint-Antoine. Sit down on a bench in a square. It's June '68 and the weather's nice. We stretch out and smoke Gauloises in the warm night.

We're wandering around swiping fruit from stalls. We've finished the Gauloises, so we pick up butts; here in Paris, there's no shortage. At night we sleep in apartment buildings, on the top floor landings where nobody bothers us, using doormats for pillows. One morning, we go into a church and hunt up the priest. "We're living on the streets," Outlaw says. "Could you give us a hand, Father?" The priest gives us ten francs and says it's all he can spare, that we should try the Salvation Army or the shelter on rue du Château-des-Rentiers. "Thank you, sir," I say, and Outlaw says, "Goodbye, Father." We buy bread and Gauloises. We reach the Salvation Army barge; it's two francs a night, but we've blown the priest's money, so we try our luck in rue du Château-des-Rentiers.

The place is free. It opens at six o'clock and we're early, so we wait. Bums wander up, drunk, and flop down on the sidewalk. One of them gives us a swig of red. He's wearing a top hat and a morning coat, his pants are so tattered, you can see his balls. He says he's a duke, a real duke, and he barfs on Outlaw's shoes. We're hungry, so we go into the shelter. We take a shower and get dusted with DDT. In the dining hall, I can't get my bread and soup down, but Outlaw asks for seconds. We sack out in the dormitory. It's full of farting, coughing, spitting, and reeks of wine, piss, and vomit. "I can't handle this," I tell Outlaw. "How about you? Are you all right?" He answers that he can't get to sleep, he's itching all over.

I'm not able to cry. I feel like throwing up.

When we step out of the shelter, I take a deep breath. A guy asks us if we'd like to eat doorbells for a while. "What's that mean?" asks Outlaw, who thinks he's in for a change of diet. The guy says he's a chimney sweep in Paray-Vieille-Poste, and he needs guys to go door to door asking people if they'd like their chimneys swept. He'll try us out for three days, he says, and feed and house us. If it doesn't work out, he slips us ten francs and it's no hard feelings. We burst out laughing at the thought of asking people if they'd like to get their chimneys reamed, but we agree. Two other bums are waiting on the sweep's truck when we climb aboard.

There are a dozen of us in the basement of the place in Paray-Vieille-Poste. They fix our grub in a huge pot and we eat it sitting on the edge of the bunks. Mornings, the sweep drops us off in some town and we ring doorbells. "Wanna have yer chimney swept?" Outlaw scores pretty good, but I don't get a single customer in three days. The guy lays the ten francs on me.

Outlaw stays on: for food and a place to crash, it's not too shabby. "So long, guy," I say. "Who knows, maybe we'll run into each other again some day." We kiss each other on the cheek.

I have just enough money for a pack of Gauloises and a bus ticket back to Paris.

II ▪

GLORIA

A HOT MORNING in late June. The bus drops me off at the porte d'Orléans. I can't decide which way to go. Then I remember the nights I spent wearing makeup on Blanche and Anvers, the neon signs, the smell of fries and pissoirs. Roland, too. I head toward Montparnasse, swipe three apples from a fruit stand. I'm walking toward the Seine, the Concorde, the Madeleine. Toward the smell of french fries and piss.

With the layer of grime I'm parading between Barbès and Clichy, I'm too filthy to cruise. A thin, pimply guy who looks familiar stops me and asks if I wasn't in Fresnes seven or eight months ago. We called him Zits because of his pimples. He stinks as bad as I do. I ask him if he knows about a place to crash. He says he's sleeping in a cellar, that I can crash there, to meet him here tonight.

So I wait. Like the washed-up, toothless old queens sputtering at each other on the benches near the pissoirs, like the mumbling skinheads looking for a handout, like the drag queens, their tits stretching skimpy T-shirts. The air's full of dust and the smell of fries; a regular country fair.

I spot a tall, balding redhead with Coke-bottle glasses wearing a blue suit, red tie, and desert boots. He walks by, comes back, smiles at me. I sit down on a bench, leaving a space between me and the queens.

"Jesus, it's hot," he says. "Hello, my name's Roger. I haven't seen you before. You from around here?"

"No, I'm just passing through," I answer. "I'm looking for a place to sleep tonight."

"You're a good-looking kid," he says. "What's your story?"

I tell him about Fresnes, Bruges, about being on the bum. He says I can sleep at his place tonight, he lives with his mother, he'll make sure she doesn't see me come in. OK, I say. It'll be better than Zits' basement.

Without stopping, Red tells me his life story. He says an Arab knifed him in a tearoom† over by Clignancourt, punctured his lungs and intestine. He used to be an office manager, but since then, he says, "I haven't been the same, haven't felt like doing anything anymore." And he tells me about his old man, dead now, that he never knew, and his asshole brother who's ashamed of him because he's a homo, and his Auntie, his mother's sister, who lives with her gay son and the son's lover, who spends his evenings sitting in front of the tube, knitting sweaters for his man. He says he's had lots of lovers, a dose of clap, and a case of syphilis.

We peel our butts off the bench and go for a stroll. He knows every queen from Barbès to Clichy: "Hi, sweetheart, hello darling. See the old queen on the bench over there? She's got an artificial anus, I bet she takes it through her false asshole. The one right next to her was a cop, one day her man shot himself and she's been a lush ever since. See the old guy walking by

† Tearoom: a public toilet used for casual homosexual encounters.—*Tr.*

who looks like a bum? That's Bread Crumbs. I don't know what he's doing on the boulevard at this hour; he never cruises. In the morning, he puts pieces of bread in the toilets. In the evening, he collects them in a plastic bag and takes them home. Then he smells them and he eats them, the filthy bitch!"

I'm hungry, Red buys me a sausage with fries. Some Gauloises, too. I puffed mine away listening to his life story.

It's night, the first neon signs are lighting up, Zits must be waiting for me. We walk along rue Dancourt, then place Charles-Dullin. Red pulls me into the hallway of a building. We feel each other up, I suck his prick, he wants to fuck me. I say no, it hurt too much the first time.

He says he likes me, wants us to live together. "Why not?" I answer. He hasn't said anything about my smell. We head toward the housing projects on boulevard Ney.

His mother doesn't notice a thing. "Is that you, Roger?"

"Yeah, mom, go back to sleep."

We fuck without making any noise so as not to wake his old lady. As I stroke his scars, he asks, "What's that on your arm?"

"A souvenir from my travels."

"Oh, yeah? Well, it's pretty gross."

"I traveled pretty far. Good night."

▪ ▪ ▪

A huge woman with red hair, screaming. "Who's this guy, where'd he come from? You've been getting buggered all night long, right next to your mother!" "He's a friend," Red answers. "He didn't have any place to sleep, he's going to stay here for a while."

"He doesn't have a job and neither do you, and you're thirty-two! You don't expect me to support you at my age, do you? I'm retiring in two months."

"Don't get upset, mom, it's bad for your blood pressure."

"Don't talk back to me, you little shit. You're killing me. And tell your buddy to go take a shower, he stinks."

I feel awkward, sitting in my tattered underwear.

All the same, she makes coffee. Red lends me some clothes and we split to go stroll the boulevards.

"Don't mind her," he says. "She's worked for twenty years in the Idéal-Standard factory, and it's made her coarse. She isn't mean, though. I know her, I'm sure she'll wind up liking you." On the boulevard, he introduces me all around. The hands I shake are damp and limp.

"This is my pal José and his Yugoslav lover Mariano, this is Bernard, his old boyfriend."

He tells José that I'm his new friend and José says, "My condolences, darling."

José does imitations of the boulevard queers: Rumble-Seat, who sits on pricks in the Barbès movie houses, her pants have zippers up the ass; the Iron Maiden, who got knocked out in a tearoom one day; some over-excited guy was banging her so hard, he slammed her head against the metal wall. She passed out in the piss, the firemen brought her around on the pavement.

José has teased hair, plucked eyebrows, and a huge silver ring with a fleur-de-lys design on his index finger. The queen of the boulevard.

I run into Zits, who wants to know what I'm up to. Just hanging out, I say. He suggests we team up, says he's into rolling rich johns. "What's a john?" I ask.

"It's a queer who pays to fuck, and some of them are really

loaded. You pick them up and take them somewhere quiet like a parking garage, and I'll wait in the garage and roll them. Sometimes you have to punch them out when they aren't drunk enough. What do you say?"

"That's not for me, man, I don't want to get sent up again. I just want to hang out."

"I get it," he says. "It's because you want to cruise the tricks for real." "What's a trick?" I ask.

"Shit, are you dense, or what? John, trick, they're the same thing!"

By day between Clichy and Barbès, by night in the three-room-kitchen-WC. Red never blows me, I blow him. His one dream is to stick his prick up my ass. I'll come around someday, he says. After he shoots his load, I jerk off.

Roger got stabbed by a sand nigger, Idéal-Standard screams. "He wanted to screw the Arab but the Arab wasn't having any, serves him fuckin' right!"

And then: "Jesus Christ, how did I wind up with a turd like him? I can't believe I was the one who crapped it!"

She likes me all right, though. "You're gonna mess that kid up," she screams. "He's too young for you. He isn't a whore. Let him go, tell him to get out of here."

I'd like to ditch Idéal-Standard, but Red says he's never left her and never will, even for a guy.

It's Sunday morning and we're in the sack when Idéal-Standard opens the bedroom door. Her eyes are red, her hair's a mess, and her huge right tit has slipped out of her bathrobe. "I'm sick and tired of seein' you in bed doing nothin' but fuck!"

she screams. "And when's that little asshole gonna get a job?"

I pull on my clothes. "I'm splitting," I tell Red. "You coming or staying?" I'm waiting out on the landing, hands in my pockets. I don't have a suitcase.

He walks back and forth between his old lady and the landing.

"Don't pay attention to her, she doesn't know what she's saying . . ."

"I've had it up to here with that fat cunt!"

"You hear the way he talks about your mother who's been feeding him for weeks now! Son, don't go off with that piece of shit!"

And the son says, "I'm leaving with you." He's crying as he throws clothes into a suitcase.

Idéal-Standard collapses onto a stool in the kitchen. She's crying and screaming, "I wanna die, I wanna die, I wanna die!"

▪ ▪ ▪

Queen José reigns over her tiny eatery in rue des Roses. The ceiling's covered with red velvet, with a lamé rosette in the center. White lace tablecloths. Bernard washes the dishes, Mariano greets the customers. Certain customers. We sleep in a booth after Queen José closes the joint up for the night. It's just for a few days.

Red finds us a place in rue Cail, over by la Chapelle. It's got a sink, a bed, a mattress, and a space heater borrowed from Queen José, who fronted us the rent money. No curtains on the window, but that doesn't matter; it faces a wall.

Red spends his days on boulevard Ney. He cleans his mother's place, does the dishes, and goes shopping. I get a job as a file clerk in a bank, but it doesn't last, just a week. I should have apologized when I bumped into the pregnant chick at the teller's window. She complained that I hit her stomach, that I didn't say I was sorry, that I did it on purpose. I hadn't noticed the chick or her stomach, but when I saw that enormous thing, I yelled, "I don't give a fuck about your little bastard, far as I'm concerned, you can both croak!" I pulled on my jacket and split.

Filing's a rotten job, it's as grey and depressing as our place in rue Cail, as the boulevard under the elevated métro between la Chapelle and Barbès. It's farther up, beyond Barbès, that the neons and the smells come alive.

I point my shoes toward the Anvers métro station, wave to the queens but don't talk to them. I've never liked talking. I wait for nightfall and watch.

From boulevard Ney, Red brings home a few groceries, sometimes a ten-franc bill.

"It's the shits," he says. "We're out of money and I can't find work because of my eyes, my eyesight's getting worse and worse." Then he takes me in his arms and says, "You mean a lot to me, but you're young. So if I want to keep you, I can't tie you down. Do whatever you like. If someone offers you food or money, go for it. Anyway, you'll always come back."

"Where would I go?" I answer.

▪ ▪ ▪

I'm leaning against a tree near the tearooms at the Anvers station. "How much?" the guy asks. Without thinking, I answer, "Fifty francs." "Don't you think that's a bit steep?" he says. "No," I say, "and the room is extra."

He's got a front tooth missing and a prole cap on his head. "We'll go to the Royal," he says, "they don't ask any questions."

The guy at the front desk gives us a form to fill out. The trick says it isn't worth it; it'll just be for a little while.

The trick puts a bill on the pillow, we strip, he stretches out on the bed. I suck his prick, but he says, "Not so fast, you'll make me come. We've got plenty of time."

He wants to kiss me. I turn my head away, say I never do that. He doesn't insist.

"You're good-looking," he says. "How old are you?" "Eighteen," I answer. He strokes me for a long time, I get fed up, I want him to shoot his wad and clear out. So I take his prick in my mouth and suck it very fast, breathing hard through my nose. He comes suddenly, and it's only the thought of the bill that keeps me from puking. We put our clothes back on without saying a word. I rinse my mouth out in the sink. I'm hungry.

I buy a sack of fries and some Gauloises.

I tell Red, "I had a guy, he laid fifty francs on me, I bought french fries and Gauloises, here's the change for tomorrow's food." He says, "You did good. And hey, you don't come cheap."

I stretch out, lay my head on his chest, I feel like talking, about anything at all. It's no use, he's already asleep.

I look for the scrap of shopping list. The number's a bit faded, it's just below *kilo of apples*.

"It's me. How are you?" She sighs. "I was worried, is anything wrong? Where are you?" I tell her I'm living in Paris with a pal, I'm working in a bank, everything's cool. I tell her not to worry about the eight months in jail, that I appeared in court and got eight months probation.

"I'm glad to hear it," she says. "Alain's out of jail. He's living in Paris on rue Poissonière. I think he wants to get married."

"So much the better. Well, here's a kiss for you."

"Here's one for you, big boy. And good luck . . ."

I straighten my hair (just like the hair in the faded photos, my only resemblance to him, and besides, I don't like my curly hair), pull on a pair of tight-ass pants, and wait, leaning against a tree. I cruise the tearooms, too. When I go to the Royal, I get fifty francs, but in garages or cars I suck for thirty, and I let the tricks fuck me when they want to.

It'll stop hurting with time, I tell myself.

Post-Office-Mimi, a retired mailman, hustles in a fake leopard-skin coat at the corner of boulevard Clichy and rue Houdon. She pals around with Big Francine who can never find a dress that fits her, and dreams of wearing red pumps, but never will, because she takes a size 12. And then there's Gloria. When a guy comes along, she starts singing opera-style: "I am Gloria, the glory of God. Fuck me, oh my lords . . ." Her very short hair is dyed blond and her hormone-fed tits stick out under a sweater that reaches to her knees. She wears high heels in Louis XV style.

I cruised a trick on their turf. "What are you doing here, sweetheart?" says Post-Office-Mimi. "This isn't your corner." "Keep the fuck away," adds Big Francine nastily. "You're bothering us." Then Gloria yells, "Cut the crap, you filthy bitches! He's my squeeze and he isn't about to steal your perverted tricks, you sluts!" "Go fuck yourselves," mutters Big Francine. Mimi says, "Shit, can't even work in peace anymore." Gloria slips her arm through mine and leads me off for a drink.

Waiting for the first neon lights to blink on, I smoke a couple of Gauloises with her in front of a kir at *La Nuit*, a hangout for hookers and their johns. Gloria's drinking like a fish, and when she gets looped, starts to tell a story about a big mansion in Neuilly, with a crystal chandelier ("like diamonds"), perfume bottles on the dresser, and minks in the closet. A white Rolls Royce with a chauffeur in a black cap drops her off at school. Sundays in the country, at Le Vésinet. Swimming pool, lawns. Travel: London, New York ("Oh those skyscrapers! Huge dicks, my pet, it was enough to make you dizzy!"). Gloria falls silent without finishing her story. From her handbag, she pulls out a photo of a kid dressed for his first Communion, with black hair and sad eyes. She says she likes the picture because of his white surplice. She starts to cry, her mascara's running.

On the back, it says, *François. La Courneuve, June 1961.*

▪ ▪ ▪

Mother's working in an old folks' home in Fontenay and Queen José drives us there in her car. She's wearing a white coat, her hair's white too. She takes the coat off and runs her hands through her hair. I introduce her to Red and Queen José: "They're friends . . ." Adoraçion is there, and I give her a kiss. "Hello, little sister!" Queen José says, "Oh, he's so cute! Hi, sweetie!" and Red says, "You have to excuse her, she uses the masculine for everything."

We don't have much to say, so Mother talks about her old folks. She likes them, she says, and sometimes she sings them old songs. She says her daughter is doing well in school, she's always first in everything in school, and her son Alain came to visit the other day, so she's happy.

Queen José sighs and winds a strand of hair around her fingers. Red plucks a bit of lint from my jacket collar.

"Are you leaving already?"

"I'll stay longer next time."

Red and Queen José are outside, waiting in the car. "I don't like your friends," she says. "I don't like their kind." "Neither do I," I answer. "I'll explain some time."

"Don't bother, I understand. I hope you're happy, big boy."

We kiss. She says, "Next time, come by yourself."

We didn't have anything to say, I shouldn't have come.

■ ■ ■

Alain's living in a room under the rooftops, it's got just a bed with a sheet.

"Hi, little bro', it's been ages. You haven't changed. Here, meet Cricri, we're getting married soon."

Cricri is a small, thin blonde. She's sitting on the edge of the bed with a Gauloise stuck in the corner of her mouth. She says hi. Alain says: "When Mom heard you were living with some guy, she really took it hard. She figured you'd wind up with a pack of kids."

I don't care for kids, I answer, what good are they? He says he hopes I'll like *his* kid, seeing as how Cricri's pregnant. "Isn't that so, Cricri?" "Yeah, I'm knocked up."

I ask him what he was doing in La Rochelle. He said he wanted to see the places where our old man lived, but couldn't remember a thing, just the boxing ring. He says: "Shit, all I found was a slab in the Saint-Nicolas cemetery, so I went out to Sainte-Soulle. There wasn't anyone at the farm, except for old Michaud. He poured Pernods and started talking. First time he's ever talked so much. Nounou'd croaked, it turns out. People around there say it was because of a broken heart because Danielle suddenly took off to go whoring in La Rochelle. Old

Nounou spent whole days crying, thinking about Danielle. She stopped eating, just shriveled up, and then one night at the hospital she puked up her life. I wouldn't have believed it, the way I'd see her hitting your 'wife' . . . There wasn't much of a crowd behind the hearse. Jacky was at sea, he's a cabin boy on some ship, and Raoul didn't want to come, seems he's studying like crazy at the La Rochelle lycée . . . Though you know, Nounou lived a pretty good life. In the twenties, she had digs in Paris on rue d'Alésia, not far from our furnished hotel. She had a high old time, all the champagne and guys she wanted, didn't do a lick of work. High-class call girl. And then one day she fell head over heels in love with some guy who split without any warning, just like that. So Nounou came back to La Rochelle, where she was born, and started doing abortions. All the wives in town came to her to get scraped out, even the police chief's old lady. The cop didn't like it, so he busted Nounou and got her two years in the slammer. Then she met old Michaud and buried herself in Sainte-Soulle in the thirties and never set foot back in Paname . . . Turns out she raised seventy kids before us, but never had any of her own. When I left, old Michaud said, 'I miss you children.' Shit, I felt like bawling. Anyway, little bro', I'll drop you a line about the wedding."

I remember, she used to talk about "Paname" sometimes. I thought it was some man.

▪ ▪ ▪

Gloria asks if I want to do a triple with her. "You'll see," she says, "there's nothing to it." The john's waiting under the neon sign of a strip joint.

We go to Gloria's place on rue Lepic. It's got a bed, a chair, a table, and on the table, empty wine bottles, pillboxes, and a whip. The white walls are bare. An enlargement of the photo of the first Communion kid is hanging over the bed.

The trick is standing there, naked. He's obese, sweating, sticky, he wants me to fuck Gloria, so I push my prick between Gloria's cheeks. Fatso's beating his meat and moaning.

"You're fucking the glory of God, aren't you?" he says. "Say you're fucking the glory of God."

"Go on," Gloria whispers to me, "say it." So I yell, "I'm fucking the glory of God, I'm fucking the glory of God." Fatso shoots his load, sobbing. He lays two five-thousand franc bills on the bed. He says, "Goodbye, my children."

Gloria says, "Good night, Father . . ."

We eat french fries and wash them down with kirs. Gloria thinks Fatso's a former priest. I don't think anything. As tricks go, he's a real sicko.

▪ ▪ ▪

Mother and I make a date to meet in a Vincennes café. She's been to the hairdresser and is wearing blue eye shadow. "How do I look?" "Wonderful," I say.

"How about my coat? I made it myself."

"It's a great color . . ." I order a kir for myself, a hot chocolate for her. It's raining out, we sit in silence. She looks at me, smiling.

She asks if I'm still drawing. I tell her that what with the gig at the bank I don't have time, and anyway, I don't feel like it. "I've started painting again," she says. "You can't imagine how relaxing it is. I paint faces I imagine. I don't like landscapes, and anyway, you have to see landscapes to be able to paint them . . ."

A man is looking at her. "I think that guy's got the hots for you." She blushes and says, "You idiot! That's all over for me. I haven't been a woman for a long time. After your sister was born, he stopped coming on to me. I tried to talk to him, but he didn't care. Anyway, you know what men are like."

I shift in my chair and order another kir. She thinks I'm drinking too much.

"You're right," I say. "Men are shits!" She bursts out laughing. "Listen to you talk, big boy!" Now it's my turn to blush. I raise my glass. "Cheers!" To her empty belly. To mine, often full.

. . .

Idéal-Standard shows up at rue Cail unannounced. She sits down on the edge of the bed and says she's sorry, she didn't want things to turn out this way, that I'm not an asshole, but a good kid. "It's no big deal," I say. "And besides, maybe I am an asshole. What do you say, Roger?" He answers that I'll shock his mother.

She retired yesterday, she says, she'll be bored, she'll be alone at Christmas. So I say, "OK for Christmas."

Red kisses me and says he adores me. When his old lady takes off, he says "We ought to get her a present." I'll manage something, I answer.

I swipe a prayer book from a shop near Sacré-Coeur, then a shawl in a Prisunic department store. I wrap the prayer book in gold paper, tie a red ribbon around it, then knot and curl the ribbon.

"It's for you," I tell Gloria. "For Christmas."

She tears off the gold paper under a neon sign. She opens the book, turns the pages, strokes it, sniffs it. Something lights up in her swollen eyes.

"It's divine," she says, "and I like the way it smells. Thanks, darling. You really are a very odd guy." She slips the prayer book in her handbag, says she'll carry it when she's hustling. We kiss. She reeks of kir and Gauloises.

There's a Christmas tree at the boulevard Ney place, with fake snow, Christmas ornaments and tinsel. Auntie, Red's mother's sister, is there, a tiny dark-haired woman (unbelievable, they couldn't have come from the same prick), and so's her son Gilbert and his lover Jean-Claude ("my sister-in-law," Red calls him). Queen José's at the head of the table. Jean-Claude calls Gilbert "darling" and serves him slices of turkey with chestnut stuffing.

Queen José's doing her imitations of the boulevard queers. Head bent over her plate, Auntie doesn't say a word, but Idéal-Standard howls with laughter. Red brings in a chocolate bûche de noël with a plastic Santa Claus stuck in it. Gilbert and Jean-Claude are feeling each other up under the table.

I give Idéal-Standard the shawl, and she gives me a belt with a big golden buckle shaped like a lion's head. "It's to keep your pants up," she says, laughing like crazy. I laugh too; I'm loaded.

I stagger to my feet, stumble, then hold out my glass of Asti and shout, "To Gloria! And who's the stupid bitch who put those tangerines under the tree? I hate Christmas tangerines!" I think I'm going to throw up.

Queen José says, "Gloria, that drunk! Is she still able to cruise tricks?"

Jean-Claude asks Red where he dragged this guy in from, Auntie mutters, "Good Lord!" Idéal-Standard brings a basin.

"You've lost weight," she says, "and you're looking pale. And you always wear those same pants, they're so tight you can see all your *equipment.* Do you go to work at the bank dressed like that?" I tell her I like these pants, they're like a second skin, and at the bank, they don't care. Down in the basement, nobody can see my equipment. "Anyway, don't worry, I'm getting by. And shit, how do you manage to smile all the time?" She says she's always smiled, ever since her parents died when she was fourteen, what else could she do?

"Sometimes it isn't easy," she says, "but you have to try, and you have to dream. I dream a lot. I close my eyes and make up colors. It's hard, but I manage. Then I try to match the made-up colors from my palette."

She pulls out her handkerchief and wipes her eyes, laughing "You big idiot, what must I look like, crying in this café? And you're drinking too much, that's your third glass in twenty minutes. Oh by the way, this package is for you. Happy new year, big boy. And buy yourself another pair of pants . . ." The package contains a pad of drawing paper, pencils, charcoal, an eraser.

Back at rue Cail, I slip the package under the bed, then walk up the boulevard to the Anvers métro.

▪ ▪ ▪

Queen José's loaned us her car for the day. Idéal-Standard fixed some sandwiches and a thermos of coffee. She wants to visit Verdun. "Don't drive so fast," she says. "You're gonna get us in a fuckin' wreck, you can barely see with those eyes of yours as it is." Red slows down. "All right, mom." He's in a good mood. "No sandwiches at lunchtime," he says. "We're taking you to a restaurant; today's a holiday." He asks if I have any money on me. I've got a little.

We pull off at a roadside cafe with paper tablecloths and steak and fries on our plates. We kill a liter of red wine with stars on the bottle. Idéal-Standard's happy. She's always dreamed of going to Verdun, she says, because her grandfather died around there in 1914.

I draw her portrait on the tablecloth. Her nose falls on a grease stain and the paper tears. It starts to rain, everything's grey, there's nothing to see. Fuck of a dream.

■ ■ ■

We're sitting in the back of a bar on place Blanche. Gloria's got the blues; in the last three days, she's turned only two tricks.

"It's my own fault," she says. "I'm always loaded. And shit, I'm tired of johns. You know what? I'd like to eat in a big fancy joint with waiters in bow ties saying things like, 'Let me take your fur coat, Madame.' And I'd like to . . ." Gloria's drunk, she's bawling.

"Stop crying," I say. "I don't want you to cry." She asks me if I love her.

"Of course I love you."

"But how do you love me?"

"Well, like a good pal. More than that, like a sister."

She says, "What if we just took off, honey? Went somewhere far away?"

I pull up my left sleeve. "Put your finger there," I say. "See, that's Rabat, in Morocco. Now go lower, you'll reach Casablanca. After that, I don't know."

She sniffles. "Shit, there isn't anything beyond that."

"Well of course," I say, "that's the Atlantic Ocean. So we take a boat, sail down here to the cape, then head back up. I don't know the places around there, but anyway, it's the Indian

Ocean. We stop in hotels that are all white, with fans in the ceilings, it's hot enough to fry your brains. We splash around in the ocean and at night, we stuff ourselves with lobster and champagne. I'm wearing a white tux with a red bow tie, you're wearing a sequined dress with your tits popping out. All right, then we go up to Egypt and head as far as Algiers—and I don't mean Barbès, either—Algiers, the white city."

She says, "What about those wrinkles, what's that?" "Nothing," I answer. "Just fucking wrinkles."

Her mascara's running, I finish my fifth kir, everything's starting to spin.

"In fac', I took a long trip yesterday, all the way to Verdun with Red and his old lady, talk about a honeymoon! It was pissing down rain, it was grey, you couldn't see a thing and there wasn't anything to see. Just think: World War I, the infantry, and nobody turning tricks in the trenches."

Gloria screams with laughter, swaying on the plastic bench with me. Now I'm crying. Gloria pulls up her sweater. She takes my head and sticks it between her tits, saying, "Come here, honey, come to mommy's breasts." She pulls down her sweater and rocks me, crooning a lullaby:

Go to sleep, little brother,
Go to sleep, little one.
You'll get milk from your mother,
When you wake, little one.

It's dark and soft and warm under the sweater. It smells good. Gloria perfumes her breasts with Rêve d'Or. The bartender throws us out.

One last blow job, late at night. The neons are still flashing. Bread Crumbs steps out of a tearoom, stooped over like a hunchback. He's carrying a plastic bag with an ad for cheap shoes on it. The bag's got a hole, it's dripping on the pavement. Bread Crumbs heads down la Chapelle, I follow him, I'm going that way. He turns into rue Max-Dormey and walks off. Coming from nowhere and going nowhere, I think. Maybe his bread has soaked up some of my piss.

Gloria thinks I've got a dose of syphilis because of the little red blotches on my face. I ask her if I'm sick, she says it's nothing. "Just a bouquet of flowers in your veins. I've already had it twice, and look at me. Do I look sick?" The tests say it's secondary syph, contagious until I get the first shot of the treatment.

I go looking for a guy who isn't a trick. I find him in a tearoom, over by la Chapelle. He says we can go to his place, his wife's on vacation with the kids. On the bed, I shove my prick between his cheeks, ream him hard, and send a shower of spirochetes into his guts. I hate kids, and I hate men's pricks.

I get my first shot tomorrow.

■ ■ ■

On the top sheet of the pad, I draw two straight lines for the boulevard, and on the right, next to the boulevard, the round tearoom. Above the boulevard, two more lines for the elevated Métro. The four lines meet: the vanishing point is toward Clichy. On the left, train tracks run toward the gare du Nord.

I imagine that it's night, which means it's grey. To get grey you have to mix black and white, but the page is white already, so I use black. A little blue above the train tracks. I rub the blue with my finger to make it lighter but it doesn't spread. It's a mess, I turn the page.

Back to Anvers. Two lines for the boulevard, two rows of trees and the tearoom (how many of them are there between Chapelle and Clichy—four, five?). It's still night. No lights on the left: the Rollin School walls. There's some light on the right: strip joints, bars, french-fry stands, so I darken the left and the middle. A bit of brown for the trees, some blue above the trees, yellow streaks for the neon signs. I spit on the paper and rub it with my finger, and wrinkled circles spread across the sheet. It looks like a kid's drawing, all straight lines, and I like curves. Maybe I didn't look carefully enough, there must be curves and colors.

She's crazy! You can't invent colors. You can't make up something that isn't there!

I stuff the pad and pencils back under the bed, and shove them with my foot so nothing sticks out.

She would have done better to buy me a pair of pants.

▪ ▪ ▪

A rumor runs along the boulevard that the Lush is dead. Nobody remembers the day she first plopped her ass on the bench; she just *was* the bench, that's all. Artificial anus is depressed. "Zip-zip," says Rumble-Seat, playing with her zipper. Zits got himself busted. His trick wasn't a trick, and he wasn't loaded either, he was a cop. Zits hauled ass from Pigalle to the corner of boulevard Barbès but the cop was faster, he slammed his face against a car. Zits collapsed without a word. He wasn't surprised, just came in second best. An unimportant rumor, a little smear of blood on metal.

In the underground garage, three levels down, I'm waiting for the john to split. I lean my head against the concrete wall, close my eyes, and think about colors very hard: white, yellow, green, blue, red, brown, black. I head back up to the boulevard.

▪ ▪ ▪

Alain stopped by to see her at the old folks' home. "I'm getting married soon," he said. So she started sewing a long white lace dress for Adoraçion.

I get a letter inviting me to the wedding in some town in the Marne. She doesn't get an invitation. She puts the dress in a box with mothballs and tucks the box away in a corner of her memory.

We take the train for the Marne, Red's wearing his blue suit and his desert boots, Queen José's loaned me a grey suit with a yellow tie. Cricri has a green dress on, her stomach is so big already, it pulls up the dress in front, you can see her skinny knees. She's wearing a white sweater and a little veil on her head.

There are seven of us at the town hall, counting the mayor. They exchange brass rings, the witnesses sign their names with X's.

Cricri and Alain are living in a trailer on a vacant lot far from town. The trailer's too small, so a farmer loaned them his barn for the reception. Cricri's folks are there, with three cousins and the witnesses. Cricri says, "This is my brother-in-law and his boyfriend."

In the courtyard of the farm we eat roast pork and drink a lot of red wine. Cricri puts on a record and tells me, "You can dance with your boyfriend, around here, we don't care." So Red and I dance a slow number together. For dessert, there are strawberries in wine in a big plastic tub. Alain's happy.

We didn't mention her once.

I promised Gloria I'd tell her everything. On the fifth kir, I describe Cricri's dress, it was very simple, with flowers on the train, and the kid holding the train wore a long, white lace dress, and there were lots of people, with bow ties and deep necklines.

"An' your folks, what were they wearing?"

"I already told you me and my brother are orphans. Anyway, a guy was playing the organ in the church, it gave everyone the shivers. Cricri could hardly say 'I do,' she was crying so hard, and you should have seen the rings: strictly low-rent. Then they took pictures on the church steps and went to eat in a big restaurant in town. Darling, they didn't have any fries, just some weird things I've never had before, I can't even tell you what they're called, and there was a huge wedding cake with a bride and groom made of sugar on top. After that we danced to a kind of oompah orchestra. I was so loaded I even danced with Red."

She says her breasts hurt because of the hormone injections.

"Shit! My big brother gets married, and that's all you have to say?"

"Don't be mad, honey, weddings always make my tits hurt."

She leans her head on my shoulder and says, "Why don't we get married, you and me?" I answer, "You must be kidding, you can't have any kids!" That doesn't make her laugh. "One more glass," she says, "and it's off to work."

On the boulevard, pieces of the night hang between the trees. I tell Gloria it's like a night made of lace. She can't hear me anymore. She staggers off toward Blanche.

■ ■ ■

A car pulls up and the guy asks if I want to get in. He looks like the Spanish teacher who slept over on the makeshift bed, so long ago and far away. I climb in. I don't tell him my price, my guts and my head are pounding with the resemblance and the memory.

We drive a long way without talking, to an empty parking lot out in the suburbs. He pulls out his prick. I put my hand on his neck, I feel like kissing this guy.

"No, no," he says. "Suck it." And he pushes my head down to his thighs. He shoots his wad. I open the door to spit, and he says, "Get out," in a hard voice. He's looking straight ahead, I get out, and he roars off. I'm standing alone in the parking lot like a jerk, with my guts and my memory. Like my satchel, set down in the pissoir.

"Have you heard about Gloria?" Fatso asks. "Heard what?" I say. "I haven't seen her in three days." Fatso tells me that Gloria took an overdose of pills, Big Francine found her body all crumpled up in the place on rue Lepic. "Poor child," he says. "I liked her, but she drank too much." He wants to make it, so we head for the Royal.

I don't believe it. She's split for Africa, I tell myself. He says, "Stick a finger up your ass, deep." I feel like laughing, remembering Verdun. World War I. Gloria in a sequined dress turning tricks in the trenches. Fatso is jerking off, he wants me to use a couple more fingers, I can't get a third one in, my ass hurts.

"I liked it when you were fucking Gloria," he says, "saying

you were the glory of God. Go ahead, say it." All of a sudden, I want a sack of fries. I can smell him sweating. Very low, I say, "I'm the glory of God, I'm the glory of God . . ."

Crying, Fatso shoots his wad.

I say, "This is the last time we're making it together, you'll have to find someone else." He says, "As you wish, my child."

I stay there on all fours, head in my hands, thinking about colors. Black. My french fries smell of shit. They taste of perfume. Rêve d'Or.

"We've been looking for you," Big Francine says. "Me and Mimi are tired of seeing you hustle on our turf. Now that Gloria's croaked, you can haul ass." And Mimi says, "Go back to your tearooms, you scumbag, you're as fucked up as Gloria was." I'm hanging on to the bar at *La Nuit*, I'm having trouble standing up. I tell Francine to go fuck herself and try to slap her one, but my fingers snag her wig, and I burst out laughing: she's bald. With her big tits and cowboy boots. She starts punching me, screaming, "Goddamned stinking faggot, I'm gonna toss this piece of shit out of here. Help me, Mimi!"

I'm lying on the sidewalk, my nose is bleeding, I can't get up. I see legs, a crowd's gathering. Then Big Francine's boot kicks me into the gutter. "Fuckin' hole!" "You pair of cunts," I yell. Neon reflections are gleaming on the wet pavement. I can't see my reflection in the gutter.

The trick gets down on all fours and says he's my dog, he'll lick my feet, do anything I tell him. "Hit me on the ass with your belt," he says.

I hit him, but not too hard. "I can't feel a thing," he says.

"Go ahead, don't be afraid." So I hit the trick's ass with all my might, I go berserk, like I want to kill him. I bring the buckle end of the belt down on his back and head, the skin bursts and blood starts to flow. "You've gone crazy," he screams. "Stop it!"

I can't stop myself, he twists away, crawling toward his clothes. He manages to escape with his clothes in his arms. I'm suffocating, there's blood on my hand and on the golden lion head.

I breathe deeply to stop the shaking. It isn't me, I tell myself, it's the boulevard. I'm sinking.

I'm finished at the Royal. They didn't like the trick's screams or his blood in the room. I don't care, I can't even get a hard-on anymore. Maybe it's the kirs. Or disgust.

Just a few blow jobs in parking garages. And no more meetings in the Vincennes café. I'm afraid she'll guess, and I don't want her to. I'm sure she was trying to tell me something with that business about imagining colors, she's always trying to tell me something but I don't get it, so on the phone, I tell her everything's cool, and hang up. I miss her.

There's a crowd at the tearoom on boulevard de la Chapelle, guys waiting to take a piss, or waiting for something else. A guy in a brown suit and green turtleneck is standing behind me. We look at each other for a few seconds. I skip my turn and go sit on a bench, and he follows. Standing next to the bench, he says, "Good evening, maybe we could go somewhere." He doesn't look like a john, so I say, "Not tonight, I'm beat." He suggests another evening. "How about day after tomorrow, same place?" The métro rumbles by overhead, and I yell, "OK, see you day after tomorrow." I go home without cruising any tricks. Red's asleep. I stretch out and think of the other guy. The one in the brown suit.

He's waiting near the tearoom in a white sports car. He's wearing a black leather coat, and his car smells good. "I was afraid you wouldn't show up," he says. I ask, "What's that smell?" He answers it's his perfume, Chanel. "My name's Stavros," he says. "I'm Greek. Why don't we go to the movies?"

It was a weird movie: this guy fucks a whole family and it messes their heads up. The mother turns nympho, the daughter wants to do herself in. The son . . . I don't remember, I was busy, I had pulled the Greek's prick out and was giving it a slow jerk. There was a scene in a train station between the father and a hustler, just a few looks, and the father strips and starts running naked across the desert. The maid floats above the house with her arms outstretched. I thought of Gloria. Maybe she's floating above some house in Neuilly, wearing a very, very white dress. A surplice. Arms outstretched.

The Greek asks me if I liked the movie, I say that I didn't quite get it, that makes him laugh, he says he'll explain it to me. We're driving aimlessly around Paris. The Greek is stroking my hand as he drives. He says he's thirty, he's a teacher, he lives with his folks in the suburbs. He also says that he's never made love with a guy or a woman, just knocked off quickies in tearooms. Then he asks, "What about you?" So I tell him about Red, about rue Cail, about hustling. He doesn't say anything, just listens. It's warm in his car, and it smells good. I close my eyes.

We drive out to La Rochelle, he parks the car near the harbor, we go for a walk. I take him to rue de La Rochelle, and say,

"See up there on the third floor? That's where I was born. I was huge, they couldn't get me out, they had to cut her, she was screaming, the blood spurted, some splashed against the wall of the little bedroom. Jojo wasn't there. He was getting loaded somewhere down by the waterfront. It was quarter to one in the morning. I was hardly born."

At the Saint-Nicolas cemetery, I show him the round photo set into the slab.

The Greek says there's a vacant maid's room over by la République. We could go spend a little time there, he says, but only if I feel like it.

We lie down on a squeaky old sofa, the electricity is off, we can barely make each other out in the dark. For a long time, we kiss without saying anything. I suck him off. He comes. I haven't dropped my trousers, it's no use, I don't have an erection. He keeps on kissing me, and then, very softly, says he loves me. I don't say anything, there's nothing to say. I feel good. He wants us to have dinner together again tomorrow. We'll meet at the same place. Near the tearoom.

The tables in the Greek restaurant have candles and white tablecloths. He's ordered kabobs and retsina. "Leave Red," he tells me. "I'll fix up the maid's room, you'll be comfortable there, and you'll forget about the boulevard." I say, "If you like."

He asks me what Red looks like, so I show him a picture of him when he was a child, in white shorts and red sandals. I don't know why, but I always carry the photo with me. The Greek wants me to burn it. I put the picture of the redheaded child in the candle flame.

I tell Red, "I've met a guy, I'm going to live with him, I'm leaving next week." He says he always knew I'd leave some day. He wants the photo back. I answer that I tore it up. "You shouldn't have done that," he says. "You don't tear up a picture of a lover when he was a child."

We don't talk before I leave. He goes to the barber, sprinkles himself with lavender-scented cologne. I pretend not to see or smell anything.

I come home one evening, there's a guy asleep in the bed, with his arms around Red. A tube of Vaseline is lying on my pillow. I smile and go to sleep, the tube in my hand.

Red never did fuck me, after all.

▪ ▪ ▪

I stuff my underwear, two shirts, a drawing pad, a box of charcoals, a set of hardly used pencils, and an eraser into a plastic bag. I leave the bedroom without a backward look. I'm nineteen years old, and then some. A lot of somes.

A white sports car is waiting for me.

▪ ▪ ▪

Little bro':

You're the uncle of a big, seven-pound girl. Her name's Cécile. I won't tell you how drunk I got with my buddies. Come see her one of these days.

We both send kisses,
Alain

III ▪

COLORS

THE GREEK REALLY fixed up the place on rue Béranger. It has everything, even curtains on the windows. "Don't work," he said, "I'll give you money, you can have anything you want."

I've quit turning tricks, just hang out all day and sleep at night. I have trouble getting used to it, it's like my head's completely screwed up. I'm into kirs and red wine. I like drinking and when I'm loaded everything gets mixed up: daylight and neon light, hustler and teacher. At times, a big emptiness. A chasm, with me comfortably at the bottom.

"Let me take you," the Greek asks, so I give him my ass. It's all I have to give, and when he fucks me, he says he loves me. I like the Greek, but not when he's fucking me.

I go looking for a tearoom. I find one on a square on rue Bretagne, and when the Greek has shot his wad and split for the suburbs, I head for rue Bretagne and I suck and jerk whoever shows up. Anybody at all, I don't look at their faces, I don't care. I let guys play with my limp prick. Not out of desire, more out of need, a need for something, I don't know what. Back in rue Béranger, I clean my mouth and hands.

On the drawing pad she gave me, I do a pencil sketch of the Greek, working from a photo. I pay special attention to the shadows. I don't spit on the paper, but blend the lines with the pencil instead. It's a good likeness, and I say, "It's for you."

He comments that I'm good at drawing and says he feels like making love.

He fucks me and leaves without taking the drawing. I slip the portrait between the sheets of the drawing pad and put the pad away at the back of the closet.

▪ ▪ ▪

The background is buttercup yellow. In the center of the canvas, a tiny man is sitting on a stool. The stool is grey and the man is blue and naked, without any details. No eyes, no mouth, nothing. In front of the man, another stool. It's empty.

The yellow is shapeless, so is the blue, the colors are reversed. Maybe the man made them up.

He has taken on the color of the made-up sky. He's waiting.

▪ ▪ ▪

She doesn't know about the Greek. I phone the old folks' home and tell her about rue Béranger. Does he work? she asks. "No sweat," I answer. "He's got a real job, he's a teacher."

"What about your job at the bank?"

"There never was any bank. I just told you that stuff so you wouldn't worry."

She says she never believed the business about the bank. "I know you inside out, and besides, a little bird tells me everything."

"Drop the little bird stuff, I'm too old for that."

"You really think you're too old? In any case, I'm happy. I really didn't like that Red guy."

Alain wrote her, there was a photo of Cécile in the envelope: a cute little girl, the spitting image of her father. Adoraçion started getting her period two months ago. Cricri's pregnant again.

She'd like to see me, she says. "In a little while," I say, "when I get it together." That's a laugh. I spend all my time getting it together.

The Greek treats me to the movies every Thursday, goes to Mass every Sunday. I go to the tearoom every night.

He wants me to meet his family. "Come to church on Sunday," he says. "I'll tell my parents you're a former student of mine."

I wait for the Greek and his parents in front of the church on rue Laferrière, not too far from the boulevard. They get out of the sports car, the Greek says: "This is my mother, you can call her Yaya, that means grandma in Greek. And this is my father, call him Papou." He says I'm a friend, a former student. I say good morning to Yaya and good morning to Papou. Any way you look at her, Yaya's a big woman, with calves twice as thick as mine. Papou's very slim and elegant, with silver hair. The Greek looks like Yaya. The sports car has only two doors, I can't imagine how Yaya managed to pry herself out of the back seat.

It's a real madhouse inside the tiny church, with people talking loudly, quarreling, kids running around screaming, with the smell of candles and sweat over everything.

The Greek and his folks light candles.

Painted wooden boards hang on the walls, they're dark and look very old, the Greek says they're icons, he has about twenty of them at home, they're very valuable. He says, "This is my brother George, and my brother Constantine, and George's wife Irene."

George looks like Yaya, he's a plumber. Constantine looks like Papou, he's studying law. Irene's pregnant. The Greek takes up the collection. (He does it every Sunday, and he keeps the books, too.) I split before the collection and have a kir in a bar while I'm waiting for him.

They invite me to eat with them out in Bobigny after Mass. Their apartment's full of gilded furniture. On the walls, there are copies of paintings in enormous gilt frames; on the windows, double red velvet curtains with woven golden cords; the tassels at the ends of the cords are gold, too.

George is reading the racing sheet with Papou, Yaya's fixing the food. Constantine asks me what degrees I have, the Greek says this is no time to talk diplomas.

We have spaghetti with some sort of weird sauce on our plates: "kima macaroni," Yaya calls it.

Papou's on a salt-free diet: he's had one heart attack already, but he puts salt on his kima macaroni anyway. Yaya notices, and chews Papou out something fierce.

I like Papou, he cheats. Yaya's a drag, but I like her kima macaroni.

■ ■ ■

I'm twenty today. Not that it matters, but I get the feeling something's drifting away.

The Greek forgot my birthday and I'm sulking. We go out to eat, he asks if I want a kir, I don't feel like drinking. He looks at me like I'm fifteen. It's fucked to be twenty.

■ ■ ■

He takes me to Greece for the summer vacation, to an island in the Aegean. We took a plane with Yaya, Papou, George, Constantine, Irene, twelve suitcases, plastic sacks, bags of groceries. When the plane took off it was like a merry-go-round. I held tight to the arm rests.

Then we took a big white ship. Everybody was barfing. I stroked my left arm. I was going far away for real.

It's Yaya and Papou's island, a pebble colored white, blue,

black, and red, where they were born. White for the houses, like cubes, all alike. Blue for the cloudless sky and the clear water. Red for the earth and the mountains at sunset. Black for the women's dresses. The Greek checks me into the hotel. He sleeps at Yaya's cube, her dowry when she married Papou. We spend our time swimming in the sea and eating kima macaroni and grilled octopus washed down with ouzo at night.

I'm getting erections, it must be the heat, the Greek goes wild. In the hotel's white sheets, my sperm mixes with my sweat. This is the country of virile men, he says. I'm burning in the sun, I've stopped thinking about the boulevard.

We take a ship for Athens. The place is a filthy shambles. The Greek wants to show me some ruins: the Acropolis, an ancient temple on a hill. He says something about an old custom, behind the temple's seventh column. "I'll explain later," he says.

It's a steep climb, I'm dying of the heat. On the hilltop, stones and tourists. The Greek pulls me behind the seventh column and gives me a deep kiss. "That's the custom," he says. "Lovers all kiss there, it brings good luck." "Talk about a fucked custom!" I say. "And let go of my hand, people are watching." I've pissed my lover off, he's pouting.

Just the same, he wants a souvenir of the two of us on the Acropolis, so we pose for a picture, sitting on a piece of column. My ass on a ruin.

▪ ▪ ▪

I'm working. In an insurance agency, the Greek's my boss. He quit the lycée to sell life insurance policies.

I'm doing a little writing to pass the time, and the agency isn't far from Vincennes park. Near the lake. There's a tearoom at the edge of the lake.

Irene has her baby: a boy. The Greek wants me to be the boy's godfather, he says I can take advantage of the baptism to join the Orthodox church, says he'd love to be my godfather. The idea of getting screwed by my godfather makes me laugh, so I say, "Why not?"

The priest dunks the kid into a basin filled with water and oil. I make the sign of the cross on the kid's forehead, someone shouts, "Long life!" the kid starts to scream. Then it's my turn. Yaya's sister Auntie Helene is my godmother. Since she can't have kids herself, she baptizes other people's kids right and left, a good dozen already, maybe more, she's lost count. Auntie Helene looks like Yaya, only bigger, with dyed jet-black hair teased very high on top of her head. She's wearing a clingy white dress open at the back and a bunch of colorful jewelry: pendants, bracelets, necklaces, rings—all fake. Auntie owns a bar near la République, she's got a ton of money, but all she likes are baptisms, marriages, and fake jewelry. The priest reads in Greek from a book, I don't understand a word. I'm supposed to say something too, but I've forgotten my lines, the Greek prompts me, it's too much trouble, he speaks the responses for me. The priest says I'm too big for the basin. With his finger, he dabs oil on my forehead, my cheeks, my chin. People kiss me, godmother says that I must call her Nana now, and the Greek says, "I'm your Nono."

Nobody shouts, "Long life!" The kid is still screaming.

There's a baptism feast at Bobigny: kima macaroni, grape leaves, goat cheese, retsina—and Nana. You can't hear anyone else. She says I'm Greek Orthodox now, I have to go to Mass every Sunday, I have to fast if I want to take communion, taking communion is very important.

With the retsina in me, Nana's starting to get on my nerves. I tell the Greek: "This is the first time you've ever been my nana†." Silence falls, Nono's at a loss for words, he says I've gotten it mixed up: Nana means godmother, Nono is the godfather.

Nono brings me back to rue Béranger. He says he's happy, his family likes me, he wants to fuck. Nono's drunk, he's reaming me hard. "Take it easy," I say. "You're hurting me." He apologizes. "Does it hurt less, this way?"

". . ."

"You realize I'm your godfather? Are you happy? Tell me you're happy."

"I'm happy you're my godfather, it's great."

Nono gives me a beautiful present: a gold chain with a cross. Very simple. Nono comes.

■ ■ ■

† Nana is Greek for grandmother, but it's also French slang for "girlfriend" —*Tr.*

Above the stony road the sky is blue with a few clouds close to the horizon, and on the horizon, a church.

A path leads from the church and vanishes in the rocky ground in the foreground. At the end of the road a priest in a cassock and round hat is standing. He's holding a camera, he's going to take a photo, he's ready.

He's waiting for the powerful, naked man to fall. There are wings attached to the man's arms, torn red wings made of paper or cloth. The lens is pointed toward the ground: the priest knows. He wants a proof of the impossible challenge. The priest could stretch out his arms to cushion the shock. He doesn't care.

On the horizon, there's nothing but the church and a few trees. And the stony desert. And maybe no film in the camera.

NANA'S LOOKING AT ME strangely. She tells me she doesn't have any children, never could. She'd like to adopt me. I answer that I'm not an orphan. I know people's looks, and hers makes no mistake. Godmother makes me uncomfortable.

Papou's dead: his worn heart gave out. I go with Nono to the hospital basement. A guy pulls on a drawer and rolls Papou out of the cooler. I want to touch the old man's skin, it's cold and hard. Like the candles in church. Everything's white: the sheet covering Papou, the guy's lab coat, the cooler drawer. Nono's crying, I'm not able to be sad, maybe it's all the white . . .

Nana's wearing a black dress hemmed with black flounces. Her jewels are black, but she teased her hair just the same. Yaya's in mourning too, wearing a scratchy black dress. Her hair's covered with a black scarf. They're sitting on the sofa, taking turns crying and screaming. Nana raises her arms and leans forward when she screams, Yaya beats her breast and tears her hair out. By the handful.

The evening of the funeral, I get very excited, and back at rue Béranger, I lick Nono all over, I'm drooling as I suck him. I jam myself on top of his prick with a moan, and come as hard as I did that night in the park so long ago, when I opened my lips to kiss a guy I'd never see again.

▪ ▪ ▪

The background of the painting is blue, dark on the left, nearly white on the right. There are four chairs in the painting.

The first one is turned toward the dark blue. A pink scarf falls from the back down over the straw seat. Spring.

The second is shown head-on, its wood a deeper yellow, and the scarf is yellow too, casually draped across the golden straw. Summer.

The third is slightly turned toward the summer, the wood is dark, the scarf is brown, neatly laid on the chair back. Fall.

The fourth chair is black, it's losing its straw, the scarf is on the ground, thrown away. The chair is turned toward the white light. Winter already.

▪ ▪ ▪

YAYA HAS FOUND A wife for Nono. Her name's Paula, she's Greek, an airline stewardess, well-educated, with very rich parents.

Paula's thirty already, she doesn't want to wind up an old maid, Nono loves kids, he's always wanted kids of his own, so they said, "All right."

It isn't a *real* marriage, Nono says. Paula knows about him and me. He says I'll be his kids' Nono, and also says he loves me. I don't understand a thing.

Yaya has fixed everything for the engagement party: coffee, Turkish delight, rose-hip jam, Samos wine. Paula's parents and Nono's family are there. Nana's sulking. She wasn't the one who found the fiancée, and marriages are her department, after all; she's already married off two nephews, three nieces, seven neighbors, and the waiter who works in her bar.

Yaya serves the coffee, then splits for the kitchen to read her prayer book. Since Papou's death, she's become very religious. The priest is there, he blesses the engaged couple, Nono gives Paula a ring, an emerald set in diamonds.

Paula's a real snob, she doesn't want Turkish coffee, she wants tea with milk. She says: "My dear Stavros, your icons are marvelous, a real treasure. And the emerald is stunning!" Paula's tall and beautiful. Paula's a pain in the butt. Nana's stuffing herself with Turkish delight, her bracelets jangling with every one she eats. She leans toward my ear, says that she's found a nice girl for me: her niece Maria, she lives in Australia, she's coming to Greece this summer, she doesn't have a dowry but she does have a beautiful trousseau, she's hard-working, she's sure to please me. I've got pieces of Turkish delight in my ear.

■ ■ ■

Nana's still in mourning, but she put on a black dress with horizontal white stripes for the occasion. I think it makes her look fat. She's sitting next to Maria. Maria's sitting beside her mother, Calliope.

Nono and I have dressed ourselves up for the introductions. I carefully straightened my hair and put on a transparent shirt with a pair of white jeans that show off my *equipment*. Nono's more low-key: a pomegranate-red shirt and pink pants. I haven't forgotten my chain and my cross. My fiancée awaits.

Nana's loaned Maria some of her jewelry: bracelets, a couple of necklaces, and a huge ring with a gigantic ball of cut crystal. She has fixed her niece's hair like hers: teased very high on top, with spit-curls on her forehead and cheeks. Maria's face has quite a few colors on it: blue eye shadow, red, almost violet lipstick, a fake beauty mark on her right cheek.

In her blue dress with yellow flowers, Calliope is smiling. She's built like Nana, only flabby. Like a blue Turkish delight. I ask Nono if she has a skin disease, he answers, "I don't think so, it must be her makeup."

Maria's small and delicate, she must take after her old man back in Australia. She's wearing a funny white dress, with a big black knot on each shoulder.

They talk among themselves. Nono translates: what a pain the tourists are, how the wind is ripening the prickly pears, the heat. We drink Turkish coffee and eat grapes. Nana winks at me to say that everything's cool.

I agree to the engagement without knowing why. Nana takes care of everything, and her cube is mobbed: the family, neighbors, neighborhood kids, Nono's grandmother who hides her money in her black stockings, looks ready to croak, and can hardly see, but can convert drachmas into dollars, francs, or marks in her head.

Nana's wearing a black dress with white feathers around her tits and one in her hair.

This time, I'm wearing white pants, a little looser than my jeans, and a very snug white shirt. Nono has on a pink shirt over pomegranate pants. Maria's wearing a tight-fitting lace dress that's splitting under the armpits, and her hair's so teased, you can see right through it. The lace is yellow.

A pope blesses us. I slip a ring, a sapphire Nono bought, onto Maria's finger. Nana hangs a chain with a cross around our necks. Both fake. She gestures to me to kiss my fiancée. I hadn't thought of *that.* Those limp lips, and all that makeup . . . Discreetly, I wipe my mouth.

We eat kima macaroni, grape leaves, and honey cakes, and drink retsina and beer. The men belch, Nana gorges on Turkish delight, I want Nono's prick. It must be the heat, or the retsina. Nono's happy. Soon we'll be cousins.

Maria goes back to Australia to pack her things. We accompany her to the pier, she walks slowly by Nana's side. Nono and I follow, on either side of Calliope.

Calliope went a bit heavy on the makeup, she's crying and the tears are wearing tracks in her cheeks, Maria's got lipstick on her teeth, Nana's wearing a twenties-style dress with fringes at the knee. We kiss. I have flecks of makeup on my cheeks and violet on my lips.

The big white ship sails off, something sparkles on the upper deck: Maria's cut-crystal ring.

. . .

Maria's at Bobigny, the wedding's a month away, I'm depressed. "I don't know what got into me," I tell Nono, "but I'll never be able to get that chick pregnant. Just kissing her makes me want to puke, so imagine what it'd be like in the sack. Do something, tell them anything. Say I'm sick, or impotent. Hey, I've got it: tell them I'm already married." Nono's in a panic, says it's a disaster, he doesn't see how he can get us out of it. I tell him I don't give a damn: "You fix it, or I'm splitting."

Nono pulled it off. He says it was so quiet in their apartment, it was like death. Maria was sitting on the sofa, crying. Nana was holding her hand, and she was crying too. It was her first failure. I ask Nono if they beat their breasts or tore their hair. He answers: "Don't push your luck, they didn't believe that story about the incurable disease. But I think Nana's found someone for Maria, an old bachelor, they could get married in two or three months."

I tell Nono: "You see, you didn't have to get your bowels in an uproar." I must be dreaming, he says. His brothers want to beat the crap out of me, even Maria's brother back in Australia wants to make the trip to give me what I've got coming.

I'm laughing, imagining Calliope with her skin disease cracking under the tears. "It isn't funny," says Nono. "Do you have any idea what kind of shit you've stuck me in?"

I like the image: Nono mired in my shit. Meanwhile, I'm finished at Bobigny. At church, too. It's no big deal, I was getting tired of kima macaroni. And I never did believe in God. That was just for laughs.

Paula falls in love with an airline pilot, so Nono breaks off the engagement and gets the emerald back.

■ ■ ■

A guy in the park, near the lake, with a plastic bag in his hand. I follow him, I want to find out about the bag.

The guy's against a tree, he takes a dildo from the bag. I spread the guy's cheeks, and gently push the thing in, it's like giving a kid a thermometer. I know the others are there, behind the trees and hedges. I slowly pump the whole rubber shaft in and out. They come closer. There's a dozen of them, maybe more. I jerk and suck them, then guide their pricks into the asshole of the guy leaning against the tree.

One guy's standing apart. He's tall and bearded, I think his eyes are blue, he isn't playing with himself, he's watching. I want him to join in. I come close and reach for his fly, he backs away. I don't understand everything he's saying.

I hear the words "morbid," "depraved," and "poor fucker."

I come back to the tree and stick the dildo up my ass.

I look up the words in the dictionary.

MORBID: related to disease; *morbid state*. Suggestive of a pathological or depraved condition: *morbid imagination*.
DEPRAVED: Spoiled: *depraved appetite*. Perverted, debauched.

I don't bother looking up "poor fucker." That one, I know.

■ ■ ■

Nono has had a phone put in at my place, worse luck.

"I phoned you last night," he says. "You weren't in, and you weren't in other nights, either."

I don't say anything about the nights spent fucking in the park. I just tell him I like nighttime, so I go out for walks.

"And anyway, I'm sick of Thursdays at the movies and sick of just being a hole to screw."

He says he loves me, that's why he screws me, I ask him why he never lets anyone screw him, he doesn't know what to say. He says he doesn't understand, he gave me everything, lifted me out of the mud. "Try to remember." I remember. Nothing's changed. Emptiness.

"Get the fuck out of here!" I yell.

I get the fuck out too. I want an ass. I run to the park.

Nono gives me his money but not his ass, and with his money, he buys my ass. I sulk for a few days and refuse him his heart's desire. He says he'll treat me to a trip to New York, it'll be a change, so I stop sulking and roll back onto my stomach.

It's dizzying, like a punch in the gut: the skyscrapers (huuuge pricks), you have to look up just to see a few scraps of sky, and at the foot of the pricks, Times Square, 42nd Street, darker than the Paris boulevards, the pavement more grey.

Neon lights, and under the lights, hustling and fucking. I want to die here, nameless, against some filthy wall covered with graffiti. Nono's afraid. He says it's dirty, it isn't safe. He wants to leave, I want to stay, we get into an argument. He doesn't understand anything, I tell him, something exists here, there's real life on these shreds of walls. He doesn't get it. He wants to know if I've been drinking, I call him an asshole and yell, "I love walls, nothing but walls!"

▪ ▪ ▪

Nono's parked his car near a tearoom. He says. "It's just to see what it's like, for fun," and asks me if it's all right. I say, "Why not?"

I wait in the car. Nono comes out of the tearoom with a guy. He says, "Why don't we have a drink over in rue Béranger?" On the carpet at my place, he fucks the guy and then touches my prick. I'm not hard. "Forget it," I say. I don't know why, but I don't like to see Nono fucking someone else. Nono's getting his rocks off. I'm in a bad mood.

▪ ▪ ▪

Nono is changing. He switches perfume: heavier, sweeter; changes clothes: less somber, bright colors, silk shirts. He takes to wearing a huge diamond pinky ring.

A red wall. A garish red, graffiti-covered wall, and against the wall, a girl, sitting on the broken pavement.

Her hair is loose and frizzy. Her face is hard, almost masculine, she has a cigarette between her fingers, a tank top, and faded jeans. She's barefoot.

The graffiti are guys' names followed by New York street numbers:

LOLLYPOP 135 SMOKY 1 BO 27 CAY 161 TONY 190
ACID IV BABY 3

A tattoo on the girl's right arm: her name, her number, and the title she's taken:

QUEEN EVA 62

Maybe she's the guardian of the graffiti, or maybe she's another wall, a living one.

Maybe she's waiting at the edge of her turf. Ready to fight.

Or the faces of CAY, TONY, BABY, *and the others.*

She's the queen of 62nd Street, but the wall is somewhere else. I don't know where.

▪ ▪ ▪

"COME OVER TO THE old folks' home," she says. "I have a surprise for you." At the home, in an empty room, paintings are leaning against the walls. Her paintings.

"This is the surprise," she says, and falls silent. Waiting. I walk around the room. Portraits of smiling women done in very bright colors, the skin of the women never pale. "That's amazing," I say. "I don't understand how you're able to do it." She says she doesn't know either, just does it by eye since she never learned how. She spends a long time finding just the right colors, she says, and when the painting's finished, she's really glad to have created something that didn't exist before. Except in her head. I tell her I could never do things like that. She says, "You couldn't do things like that: you could do much better . . ."

A tiny overgrown garden, a garden gone to seed with a pond, and in the middle of the pond, a plaster angel.

The pond's full of very dirty water with lily pads floating around the angel. An old shack at the end of the garden. I found the address in a suburban phone book: *Mademoiselle Chameron. Drawing, pastel, and painting classes.*

She doesn't even come to my elbow, she's thin as a rail, with stiff grey hair. There's a little bump on her shoulder blade, and little bumps on her fingers too, they're twisted every which way. Mademoiselle is as old as her shack, but her eyes are very blue. She smiles all the time and never raises her voice.

Her studio is a total mess, with easels everywhere and on the wall, plaster busts and Mademoiselle's canvases. They're huge, full of color, bouquets of flowers, landscapes, gardens, woods. The pond with the angel, in sunlight, in the snow. The angel head on, in profile, from the back.

She gives me a few charcoals and a rag, a sheet of paper, and sets me up at an easel. She takes down a plaster bust of a crying child. At times, she corrects a shadow, a line, a curve. You have to create color with black and white, she says. Shadow, light, modeling, her crooked pinky on the crying child's face.

Voltaire, Carpeaux's *Negress*, a gladiator, a nude bather; Mademoiselle's pleased with me.

I buy a box of pastels and some Ingres paper, Mademoiselle sets three vases on a table.

She alters a shadow, a curve, the light falling on a piece of porcelain. She says, "We'll make something of you if the little piggies don't eat you first." What if I was the piggy?

I cover the vases with glass and frame them in wood.

At the old folks' home, I say, "This is for you, for your birthday." She tries to keep from crying. Says she's going to put the vases above the sideboard in the dining room.

Cricri has her baby. Another girl: Alice.

▪ ▪ ▪

We've quit going to the movies on Thursday. We hang out in cafés or gay bars, drinking whiskey, lots of whiskey. I like it, it gets you loaded faster than kir or wine. I stand at the bar. Nono buys rounds for the thirsty guys who don't have the price of a drink. Nono's very generous.

Nono neglects his heart's desire, comes to my place in rue Béranger only occasionally, with company. I watch and wait to change the sheets.

When the butt-hole of the evening leaves, Nono always stuffs a bill in his pocket.

Nono's getting fat and bloated. He says he's making up for

lost time. He's wrecking his life and I like Nono's wrecked and bloated life. He's starting to look like me.

But Nono says he loves me, and then I don't understand.

I buy a couple of tubes of paint, three brushes and two canvases. I paint three heads sitting on rocky ground, the eyes are empty, the tops of the skulls chopped off. The sky fills the heads, spills out of the tops of the skulls.

I close my eyes, imagining the colors. I mix the colors by eye, hesitate, then spread the mixture on the white canvases. Nono hoots with laughter. He says I'm no Leonardo yet. "Who's this Leonardo?" I ask. "Another one of your guys?"

"Leonardo da Vinci, you ignoramus, and anyway, this stuff's morbid, I'd never hang anything like that on my wall."

I feel like slapping him, but Nono's right: it's worthless and morbid. I'm going to quit seeing Mademoiselle. It's no use. I slash the canvases.

Nono has a lover, a tall, dark Tunisian. His name's Lucien, but Lucien's dirty and he stinks, so I nickname him Lunch-bucket.

He's no rent-a-hole who leaves with a bill stuffed in his pocket, but a live-in lover Nono has set up in a place on rue Charlot, not far from rue Béranger. Every evening, Nono goes to rue Charlot. Nono buys a blue Porsche to drive Lunch-bucket around in.

He says Lunch-bucket just got out of jail, three years for a heist, so he's helping him out. "But there's nothing between us, you know. He's just a pal." Nono's shitting me, so I yell, "A pal, my ass! A paid hole for you to screw, that's what he is! You gonna baptize him, too? Why don't you become a Muslim, that way you can get fucked by your godfather. Don't you think that's a good idea?"

He says I'm out of my head. Could be, I've a fair amount of whiskey sloshing in my gut. I slam my fist into Nono's face. He doesn't react. I want him to say something, to scream, or to hit me, but Nono doesn't say a word. His eyes are elsewhere.

I open another bottle of whiskey and pour us a couple of glasses. Nono's eye is red. Here's to Nono's red banner.

Lunch-bucket isn't faithful, he screws girls and says he doesn't give a shit for that fat Greek faggot, just wants to fuck his money and get driven around in his Porsche. Lunch-bucket's vulgar.

Nono finds out that Lunch-bucket's cheating on him with girls, and that's something he can't stand. Nono can't abide girls. He's unhappy in love, so he drinks. I drink too. To forget Nono and his faithless Lunch-bucket.

Marie lives on rue Béranger. We often hit the local bars for drinks together. Marie's thirty, she has very wide shoulders and huge tits that cry out for a bra, but she's too ashamed to go into a store and tell them her size, so she lets them go. Her nose is crooked, she doesn't have any lips, and she's got gaps between her teeth. All of her teeth. Marie's legs are very thin, no calves at all.

Summer and winter, she wears black pants and a cape with a huge collar turned up to hide her face. Marie isn't just ugly, she's monstrous. She knows it and doesn't care. She has only one dream: getting pregnant.

Lunch-bucket's always saying he'll screw anything that

moves, even a skeleton with hair. Monstrous Marie says she can't find any men to fuck her and get her pregnant.

"She's a bit ugly," I tell Lunch-bucket, "but very nice, it's a clean shot with no problems."

To Monstrous Marie, I say, "He's tall, dark, and good-looking, it ought to work, let me know when you're ready."

I change the sheets on the bed and fluff up the pillows. I needn't have bothered. Monstrous Marie just stretches out on the carpet, waiting. Lunch-bucket walks into the apartment smiling, but then his smile freezes.

I give Lunch-bucket a drink to loosen him up. The whiskey does him good. I kiss Monstrous Marie on the mouth and suck on the ends of her enormous breasts. Lunch-bucket drops his pants and plays with his prick, trying to get a hard-on. No dice.

My tongue between Monstrous Marie's thighs.

That does the trick. Lunch-bucket gets hard.

Monstrous Marie cleaned her crotch with a cheap towelette, and my tongue's stinging. I split for the bathroom, wash out my mouth, and wait.

▪ ▪ ▪

I'm staggering between the trees in the park. I don't feel like barfing, but I can hardly stand up. I lean against a tree and let myself slide to the ground.

They come. I don't know how many. They're a blur. A merry-go-round in my head. A country fair.

Hands on my body, pulling off my clothes.

It must be cold, but I don't feel anything.

Just a pain between my legs.

My memory leaves me. Coma.

▪ ▪ ▪

A damp, silent morning. On my skin, whitish flecks. They left me my pants. I can't find my jacket.

A little blood between my legs. Above all, don't bawl. Just hate yourself.

▪ ▪ ▪

The syphilis is back: secondary stage. Nono hasn't fucked me in ages. Too bad, I would have loved to shoot him a few spirochetes. Just a couple of them, like a secret between me and the syph.

I'm sinking. I'm hanging on to Nono so as not to sink, but he's sinking too. I don't know if I'm dragging Nono down or if he's pushing me under. It must be me, I fuck everything up, I've never been anything but a fuck-up, except that Nono seemed tough enough in the beginning. Solid. I could split, strike out on my own, but where to? The boulevard? At times, I miss the boulevard. I didn't hang on to anything there, it was simpler.

And that butt-hole Tunisian, he must be a butt-hole, Nono never lets anyone jump him, so he's the one fucking that rotten hole. I'm sure his hole is dirty, I used to wash my hole when Nono jumped me. Even on the boulevard I kept my hole clean, except at the end, when I was selling myself at a discount.

I'm just a piece of trash. Those goddamned waves of fear in my gut, day and night, that hit without warning and why am I bawling for no reason, I can't stop bawling, why are my hands shaking?

I tell the doc everything: Nono, the fear, the tears, the shaking, my brains dribbling out my prick. He doesn't have any answers, just drops and pills. With the whiskey, they make a great cocktail, I walk around in a daze, and in my head, things between Nono, Lunch-bucket, and me calm down a little.

Monstrous Marie's pregnant. She's happy, almost pretty. She asks if I want to be the kid's godfather. I howl with laughter, but don't turn her down, just say, "We'll see." I ask her over to rue Béranger for a drink.

I've bought champagne, cookies, and a green plastic apron with pink flowers. Monstrous Marie, Nono, and Lunch-bucket are sitting on the carpet. I didn't tell Nono and Lunch-bucket there'd be four of us, and a heavy silence fills the place. I put on my apron and busy myself in the kitchen: cookies on a plate, four glasses on a tray.

The cork pops, the champagne spurts. I titter as I pass the cookies, Nono asks what we're celebrating, Lunch-bucket looks pale, Monstrous Marie's packing it away, I tell her it's good for what ails her. I put an old 45 rpm on the record player: Lucienne Boyer, *Plaisirs d'amour,* I adore that record. I serve the champagne and tell Nono that in a few months, he's going to be a Yaya.

I tell Nono about sucking on Monstrous Marie's tits, about having to give Lunch-bucket a jump-start, about the cheap towelette.

Nono looks at Lunch-bucket. A dirty look. He gets up and splits without a word, Lunch-bucket follows him like a puppy, his tail between his legs. I think that between Nono and Lunch-bucket, the shit's about to hit the fan.

Monstrous Marie says she was a bit embarrassed about the

towelette. She also says my buddies are weird. Monstrous Marie has cookie crumbs between her teeth. I raise my glass: "To Yaya!"

The shit must have hit the fan, because I don't see Lunch-bucket or the Porsche on rue Charlot anymore. Nono's pissed off, he didn't much like my little scene, but then I become his favorite again. Or rather his lady-in-waiting in the cafés and gay bars. Nono's gigolos, Nono's diamond glittering under the neons. And his fixed, drunken stare. Something's eating him.

I kiss Nono in the car, I suddenly want him, my hand's on his fly. He pulls my hand away. "Don't bother, I can't get it up anymore."

Nono's prick is dead. His lips are, too.

He's leaving for the Caribbean in a few days, alone. "To relax and think," he says. "I'm going to miss you, I'll write." A strange glint in his staring eyes.

A letter from Martinique. The weather's heavy, wet and hot. He's thought it over, he wants to start all over again, like in the beginning, we'll talk about it when he gets back. He also writes that he loves me. Stavros.

It's early in Point-à-Pitre, maybe six in the morning, I ring his hotel room.

Lunch-bucket answers. "We went to bed late last night, he's sleeping, I don't want to wake him."

I'm on all fours on the carpet, holding my head, screaming. Just screaming.

He brings me a souvenir from the tropics, a machete in a leather sheath. He doesn't mention the letter, I don't feel like screaming anymore.

Dropping my pants, spreading my legs. Giving my mouth and my ass. A whirl of come and shit, stains to help me forget myself.

At rue Béranger, I stagger up the stairs. I want a long night without any memories. I stretch out on the carpet, one last cocktail. Coma.

▪ ▪ ▪

The dirt in the background is a smooth burnt umber. At the bottom of the canvas, in the center, a skull. It doesn't have any teeth, it seems to be smiling.

Hanging in the empty eye socket is a medal, the croix de guerre. *The medal isn't important, I could have painted something else: a bank note, a photo, or nothing.*

Or written someone's name on the yellowish forehead.

■ ■ ■

SHE RAISES MY PILLOW, says she's been coming for three days but I've been asleep. She sits in a chair, lays a hand on the white sheet. She asks if I'm having problems. I don't have any problems, I just don't feel like myself.

"I know, big boy, it isn't always easy, but plenty of men manage to get through life."

"I'm living all right, it's not that I'm not myself, it's more in my gut, you know, like a big emptiness. It started back on avenue du Maine. With Red, I didn't think about it so much, and then it came back with the Greek, so I did some filthy things, dirty stuff, disgusting things, to take the place of something, I don't know what. You probably don't understand, but I don't have the words to explain it any better."

She understands, she says. She's felt that big emptiness in her gut, too. When the Spaniard used to hit me too hard, she didn't think about herself, she thought about us.

"When things go wrong, think of me," she says. "And don't worry, you'll love someone one of these days, we all fall in love some day. Be patient." How does she know I've never loved anyone?

She's stroking my hand gently. She says, "Try to want something, try really hard."

She kisses me on the forehead and says she loves me. Outside, the sunshine's beautiful. Spring sunshine. She'll come back tomorrow.

The Greek's waiting in the Porsche. We don't speak, I let the sun wash over my face through the window.

We're at a red light, his hand's on my neck, I get out of the car, I don't want his hand on my neck anymore. Or anybody's hand. I want to walk by myself, wherever I want to go. There are colors on the people, on the walls, too. Even the grey of the sidewalks isn't grey.

Empty my head, close my eyes, make something up. Create something that doesn't exist anywhere: on the canvas, a yellow background, and in the middle of the canvas, a little blue man, sitting on a grey stool.

Lunch-bucket's getting married soon, to a girl he met in the Caribbean, the Greek's found another guy, a piece of meat over by Pigalle, Monstrous Marie's left for Spain to deliver her bastard in the sun. Shreds of lives, four chairs on a blue background.

I tell the Greek: "I'm splitting, going somewhere else. A studio in a little street near a train station." What will I do for money, he wants to know, what do I plan to do in the studio?

For the money, I answer, "My mother."

For the rest, I don't say.

▪ ▪ ▪

On the big canvas, it's like a procession. A fat woman in a black dress with her hair in a black bun. Behind her, a kid in a grey smock. He's walking, head down, wearing a dunce's cap. Pinned to his chest, an open notebook.

The sky is yellow, the village houses brown. There are only three colors in the painting. Almost like a sepia photo. A dog is sitting on the right, watching the kid and the fat woman in black. The dog is a bastard.

The kid is older. He's sitting on a staircase, a grey rag in his left hand, the one holding a banister post. His right hand rests on one of the steps. The staircase turns and the banister disappears toward a light. Perhaps an open door. The walls are brown, very dark, the staircase too. The kid's skin is white: face and knees. He is looking at me.

The kid is leaning against a wall, hands behind his back. He is in profile, watching the muscular man in the white shirt. The man is shown head-on, clenching his fist as he looks at the kid.

A hard look.

The wall is a dirty yellow. Scraps of wallpaper.

A dim light between the kid and the man illuminates the fist. The kid's look is a challenge.

The night is an uneven, very dark blue. Scraps of night. On either side of the canvas, jagged black shapes. Along the shapes a few yellow dots spell out a word: HOTEL.

A background without depth, colors without color: a wall. And graffiti on the wall: PEACE IN VIETNAM, US GO HOME, CHARONNE I HATE LUNCH-BUCKETS—PROLES—SCUMBAGS.

There's a crack in the wall, a black crack.

The kid must have blackened his fingers on the cracked wall.

He is probably about fifteen. He is lying on a board, wearing a grey outfit, barefoot, his eyes closed. He isn't sleeping, he's dreaming. His right hand is slipped into his open pants. The canvas is rectangular, very tall, the kid is lying at the bottom of the rectangle.

A light high on the cell wall lights up the kid's hand.

Another wall, pale, evenly lit. A cell. The kid is in profile, wearing a white shirt. Behind him is another kid, older, black leather jacket. His face is hard, he is undressing the kid in the white shirt.

They don't look alike, but they know each other.

An exchange in black and white. Maybe a confession.

The bodies are lit up, the background is dark. A bit of white sheet. Wrinkled.

From the back, the man has wrinkled skin, white hair, he is fucking the kid. He seems to be fucking the kid, the kid is grimacing, it hurts. It looks like a fight, but it isn't. It's an initiation. The bodies are pale, but the kid is wearing makeup.

It's night. Blue, almost black. In the foreground, the kid, head-on. Behind him, a man wearing a cap. You can't see his face, it blends into the night.

The kid's face is lit only from one side. A sideways glance. He knows the man is behind him, the man is about to speak, suggest something.

The kid is waiting, he knows what the man is going to suggest.

In the depths of the night, hanging on the night: yellow, blue, and white dots, straight lines: neon lights.

ABOUT THE AUTHOR

Denis Belloc was born in La Rochelle in 1949. *Neons*, first published in France in 1987, is his first novel. Since then, he has completed *Suzanne* (1988), *Képas* (1989), and *Les aiguilles à tricoter* (1990).

ABOUT THE TRANSLATOR

William Rodarmor is a magazine editor in Berkeley, California. His book translations include *The Carnivorous Lamb*, by Agustin Gomez-Arcos (Godine, 1984) and Denis Belloc's *Képas* (Quartet Books, London, 1992).

NEONS

was set by NK Graphics in Keene, New Hampshire, in Bodoni Book, a typeface named after Giambattista Bodoni (1740–1813), the son of a Piedmontese printer. After gaining renown and experience as superintendent of the Press of Propaganda in Rome, Bodoni became head of the ducal printing house in Parma in 1768. A great innovator in type design, his faces are known for their openness and delicacy.

This book was printed and bound by R. R. Donnelly and Sons in Harrisonburg, Virginia. Book design by Lucinda Hitchcock.